Fae Wings
and
Hidden Things

A Wolf Pack Publishing Anthology

Contents

LUCK

Warren Rochelle

Walking home down Tate Street on the last day of classes Glosson Bennett always felt lighter. By the time he turned off Tate onto Carr Street, he felt as if with just a little effort he could take flight or simply just rise upward until he found a comfortable bit of sky in which to float. The neighborhood, College Hill, would spread out, and the UNC Greensboro campus, a green island, and over the city he would drift.

Never mind the box of undergrad intro fiction portfolios he was carrying. And never mind all the grading he had to do after that. Today classes were over. No matter how well his classes had gone, Glosson always found himself longing for this last day a month before the semester's end. That he and Cameron were heading to the Old Town Draft House for a drink and then dinner out made it all the sweeter.

Glosson was upstairs changing out of what Cameron called his professor costume when he heard the door opening and voices. *Who are you talking to, Cam? Tell them you're busy, okay?* Glosson quickly pulled a blue and gold UNCG T-shirt over his head (part of his last day costume), hoping he could get rid of whomever it was before Cameron got too involved in what was probably some random and accidental conversation. That Cameron seemed to have never met a stranger was something Glosson both envied and found endearing, and sometimes, annoying. He had been looking forward to their semester's end drink and dinner all day long and whomever it was could go hang. *Cameron, please, stop talking...*

When he got downstairs to the front door, Cameron was standing there, still in his school counselor costume, talking to a man and woman who looked vaguely familiar.

"Glosson, there you are." Cameron took his hand and gently pulled him out on to their front porch. "You remember Peter Macnab? Peter, Owen and Elspeth's son? Peter's wife, Sarah? We met Christmas before last."

Of course. He remembered Peter and Sarah now. Owen and Elspeth Macnab, Peter's parents, both retired professors from nearby Greensboro College, were their next door neighbors. Or they had been. Glosson and Cameron had been house-sitting and looking after Lord Donalbain, the Macnabs' rather large and curmudgeonly black cat, for almost two months. The Macnabs, junior and senior, had gone off to Scotland and Wales together. Owen and Elspeth had both grown up in Killin, a small town in central Scotland. The original plan had been for two weeks in Scotland and a week in Wales, then London. Cameron got an email from Peter in the second week. His father had taken ill in Killin, would they mind ... Then, the next email, ten days later: Owen Macnab had died and Elspeth wasn't coming home, *we are so sorry, would you mind looking after Lord Donalbain a little longer and the mail ...*

Peter looked just liked his mother, the same red hair and grass-green eyes. "I'm so, so sorry," Glosson said, taking the man's hand. Owen and Elspeth had been great neighbors and friends. They had asked Glosson and Cameron over for afternoon tea right after they moved in. Elspeth made amazing scones from scratch. Meals every now and then, mostly random chatting on the street when coming home from a neighborhood walk, catsitting Lord Donalbain, collecting mail. Both Glosson and Cameron adored their Scottish accents and had spent too much time trying to imitate them and had watched way too many instructional YouTube videos on how to speak like a Scot.

"Mum insisted he be buried there in Killin, surrounded by the ancestral territory of the Macnab clan. It took us forever to arrange things for the funeral, thank goodness they both had kept their UK citizenship. Mum said she wasn't leaving him alone, so we had to get her settled there. But finally we can take care of the house," Peter said. "We imposed so long on you guys and we wanted to thank you in person, and Mum wanted you to have something as a thank you."

Cameron shook his head, as he waved his hand. "You didn't impose. We were glad to do it. We always liked your folks."

"Lord Donalbain was no problem," Glosson added, wondering where the black beast was at the moment. Lord Donalbain liked to wander and hide in various corners of their house, or go next door and curl up on the porch swing. Sometimes he saw the cat methodically patrolling the Macnab yard, walking from corner to corner.

Sarah held out what looked like a tiny treasure chest, the size of a music box. Cameron took it, turning it this way and that. Glosson wanted to touch it, trace the curious carvings that looked like Celtic knots. "She insisted it be this box, for luck. She didn't give us a key. She said we had to make sure the realtor touched it first, then give it to you. We got an offer this morning, even before the sign went up, so I guess it works. She wanted you two to have some luck."

Peter looked down at his feet and then back up, first at Cameron, then at Glosson. "And we wanted to ask you guys if Lord Donalbain could just stay on here? What with quarantine and stuff, it would be impossible to take him over there, and he likes you guys. There's some extra food Mum and Dad had and Lord Donalbain's got a box of toys that I can bring over …"

"Sure, we'll take him. Bring over his toys," Cameron said quickly, looking apologetically at Glosson, who nodded, hiding a frown.

"I guess we have a cat, then. Let me get you the mail we collected." *It's okay, but we really should have talked about it. You do this to me all the time, Cam.*

Much later, that night, curled up in bed, spooned together in the close darkness, Cameron apologized. "I know, I know, we should have talked, but we both like Lord Donalbain, and we've talked about getting a cat. Sorry, Gloss."

Glosson sighed. He could never stay mad at Cam for long. He pulled Cameron against his chest, stroked his white-blond hair. "You're forgiven. Where is that beast, by the way, and where'd you put that treasure chest? Did you get it open?"

"On the counter by the kitchen sink—" Before Cameron could finish answering, the cat screeched and something hit the floor, breaking.

"What the hell?" Glosson scrambled out of bed, with Cameron right behind him. The treasure chest lay on its side on the counter, open and empty. The shattered remains of a coffee mug littered the floor. Lord Donalbain crouched on top of the refrigerator, hissing, his fur and tail up, his bright yellow eyes almost glowing.

"Donal-boy, what are you hissing at? You knocked the mug off. I hope to God you didn't see a mouse," Glosson said, frowning at the cat. "I'd get you down but picking up a pissed-off cat when naked is not a good idea. Cam, what are you doing?"

Cameron had turned on all the lights. He stood by the dining table, scanning the room. "I thought I saw something, like a shadow moving."

Glosson yawned. "It was a shadow moving; it's the middle of the night. Let's clean up this mess and get back to bed. Watch your feet C'mon. Leave his lordship up there. He'll come down when he's ready. I thought that box couldn't be opened."

Cameron stood staring a moment longer, then shook his head and grabbed a broom. "Yeah, me too. But I did wish it open a while ago, too." He yawned.

A little while later, they tumbled back into bed.

Glosson was up long before Cameron. The box of portfolios to grade, then, back to his office, drop off the completed box, grab the to-be-graded box, and keep grading like a maniac, post grades, and then. That. Would. Be. It. His grad fiction workshop, already done. He staggered into the kitchen to tank up on caffeine and scrounge for an English muffin and stopped and stared. Lord Donalbain was still on top of the refrigerator, clearly still upset about something. And on the counter by the sink, all the dishes from the drainer, arranged in stacks. *What the fuck, Cam? Got bored putting up the dishes?*

Glosson shook his head. "I'll feed your lordship, but you have to come down and get it, or I am shipping you to Scotland, quarantine or no quarantine…"

A while later, he looked up from a depressingly bad short story when he felt Cameron coming down the stairs.

"Hey. Good morning. Almost done?" Cameron stood in the doorway, scratching his stomach. His white-blond hair stood up in odd places, like tiny tufted horns.

"Five more. Did you leave all the dishes out on the counter?"

Cameron shrugged. "Sleepwalking, I guess," he said over his shoulder as he disappeared into the kitchen. Glosson heard the refrigerator door open. "You know, I had really weird dreams. I think I'm going for a bike ride. Any coffee? Hey, there's a twenty-dollar bill on the floor. Yours?"

"Something you ate, I guess. There's still some coffee in

the pot. You might have to nuke it. I'll finish up this box while you're gone. Finders keepers on the twenty."

Later that morning Glosson couldn't find his keys when he was ready to take the graded portfolio box to campus. He finally found them in the medicine cabinet in the bathroom. *How the hell did they get here? Cam?* He heard Cam coming in downstairs a he stared at the key.

"Did I do what? Hide your keys in the medicine cabinet? Yeah, right, Gloss. No, it wasn't *me.*"

Something about Cameron's face made Glosson give up trying to get Cameron to admit to that prank, never mind leaving the dishes out. It just wasn't worth it.

On Thursday, the last of his grades posted, Glosson came home after lunch with his next door office neighbor to find his lordship perched this time on the dining room table, verboten territory. Dishes had been stacked on the counter again. After spending over an hour looking for his car keys to run an errand and finding them in the refrigerator on top of the butter, Glosson had had enough. No more pranks.

"What? You think I'm doing what?" Cameron turned from hanging his shirt in the closet in their bedroom to glare at Glosson, who had been waiting all afternoon to have it out. Glosson glared back. "Cameron, you're driving me crazy, one thing after the other, hiding my keys. You're driving Lord Donalbain crazy too. Enough with the jokes, okay?"

"Nothing is wrong with me, and I'm *not* doing any of whatever the hell you're talking about. *You* might want to explain the flowers delivered to school today. You *didn't* send me a dozen yellow roses, yeah, right. I'm not picking on the fucking cat. And here I was feeling all romantic and you're accusing me of being some adolescent practical joker?"

Glosson clenched and unclenched his fists. "I didn't order any roses."

"And I haven't been hiding your fucking keys."

"Somebody did."

"It wasn't me. If it was anybody, it was—never mind. Maybe you just forgot—you ever think of that?" Cameron jerked a t-shirt over his head and stormed out as Glosson stood at the top of the stairs, yelling for him to come back and talk.

Later Glosson blamed it on stress and apologized. Cameron grudgingly accepted. They both apologized to his lordship. After the make-up sex, they laughed about how silly each other had been and managed to talk about where they would go for a getaway, once Cameron's school was out and he was done with counselor paperwork at the end of June. Some things, Glosson thought, as he mentally pushed away unanswered questions, should just be left alone.

Things were okay for a good while.

Glosson had the house to himself while Cameron was at school and with a pot of coffee he settled down to work on his novel every morning. The moderate success of his first novel had helped him get the job at UNC Greensboro, but that had been two years ago. It was just him and Lord Donalbain, the novel, and coffee. Sunlight poured into the study. Through the open window, he caught the scent of gardenias from their back yard. The outside noises faded and all he could hear were his fingers on the keyboard.

Glosson let himself mostly forget the weirdness with the keys until one Saturday night the last week of May. That afternoon, the movers had emptied out the Macnab house and he, Cameron, and Lord Donalbain (snuggled in Cameron's arms) had said good-bye to Peter and Sarah. A veggie lover's pizza from Slices up on Tate, and beer for dinner (paid for by Cameron; he had found three twenties while biking in the neighborhood...), a walk, sex, and later, as they snuggled, drowsing into sleep, Glosson felt somehow things were back to normal.

The bed collapsed just after midnight. Glosson woke up screaming, sure there had been an earthquake. It took Cameron several minutes to calm him, holding him close in the ruins of their bed. Neither one wanted to get up and go into the guest bedroom; it was just too much trouble.

"Are you sure you're okay with me going off biking? I mean, there's a bed upstairs to repair," Cameron asked after he had poured himself a second cup of coffee Sunday morning. He was meeting a few of his counselor buddies for a bike ride in the country, a jaunt planned weeks ago.

Glosson looked at his tall, white-blond husband and nodded. "Probably not much we can do anyway, other than buy a new bed, given our carpentry skills. Oh, did you get up really early and eat and go back to bed? I found a bowl in the sink. Oatmeal?"

"Yeah. More of those weird dreams. So I woke up early, ate something. I should have cleaned it up. I'm sorry. After I made it, I didn't really want it," Cameron said as he fished a carton of almond milk out of the refrigerator for his coffee. He looked at Glosson and shrugged. "Well, if you're sure, I'll go. And will you stop hissing?" The last remark was directed at Lord Donalbain who was back on top of the refrigerator. Except for coming down for food and the litterbox, and to get one of them to let him outside for yard patrol, his lordship was not spending a lot of time actually touching the floor.

"New shoes and socks?"

Cameron looked down and nodded. "Yeah, I guess I'm getting absentminded. I found an envelope with cash stuffed in it in my sock drawer. Decided to splurge." Cameron looked down again. "Uh, there is something I've been meaning to tell you—" He paused and shook his head. "Never mind."

"Give me a kiss and go." He swallowed his dream question. Glosson had asked about the weird dreams more than once, but Cameron refused to talk about them. Later, he said.

Glosson delayed dealing with the broken bed until later in the morning. He grabbed their toolbox before heading up stairs. He stripped off the bed linens and wrestled off the mattress, pushing it up against the wall. When he started to examine the bed legs, he froze. *It can't be. No. Oh my God.* The bed legs had been sawed through. Glosson ran downstairs and out onto their porch and across the back yard to the tool shed. Found the saw. With bits and shreds he recognized as coming from the spread on their bed. He ran back inside and checked the spread. Torn and ripped. *Cam's trying to—no, we were both in the bed. Cameron's going crazy. I don't know what to do. I don't know who to call.* He wished, wished he was still in therapy. He wished he lived closer to home and that his mother was still alive. He wished he lived closer to his best friend from high school; he wished he was closer to people at UNCG.

Glosson was sitting at the top of the stairs when Cameron came home at twilight. He heard the back porch door open and hugged himself, hoping he was going to be brave enough. When Cameron came inside, his bike in its place on the porch, he called out for Glosson.

"Honey, I'm home! Would you believe I found another twenty? Starting to like ol' Andy Jackson."

Glosson waited a beat too long to answer. "Up here."

Cameron stood at the foot of the stairs, one hand on the banister, the other holding his bicycle helmet. Then he bounded up the stairs and sat down by Glosson. "What's wrong? Did something happen? Is somebody sick?"

"I don't know what to do. This is beyond me." Glosson broke down with his face in his hands and wept. Cameron pulled him against him, murmuring it was all right, it was going to be all right, until Glosson pulled away and faced him. "The bed. The bed legs were sawed through. Bits of the bed spread are on the saw."

"You think I did it."

"I don't know what to think. Maybe we should go see a doctor."

Someone laughed, a thin, high laugh. Glosson jerked back, pressing himself against the wall. "Are you laughing at me?"

"You heard that? Oh, thank God, I thought I was going crazy. It's *him*, he's doing all this—the bed legs, the dishes, the things he told me in the weird dreams, everything."

"*Him?* Him who? Told you in your dreams?"

Cameron pointed behind Glosson to the door to their bedroom. He turned and there, leaning against the doorjamb, was a very small creature, no bigger than a house cat, with a wrinkled human-appearing face, and thick brown curly hair all over its body. It waved at the two of them, and then extended what looked like a six-fingered hand and blew a kiss.

Glosson could actually see it, a tiny red valentine in the air, and he stared as it flew toward Cameron. He watched as Cameron grabbed his helmet, swung, and the valentine shattered, red dust sprinkling on the floor.

"Do you see him? Did you see what he just did? He's been in all my weird dreams," Cameron whispered. The creature's hair shifted from brown to white-blond, the same color as Cameron's, and it pulled a pouty face.

Glosson nodded. "I saw it. What is it?" Even with an impossible creature staring at them, Glosson had never felt more relieved.

"Thank God. I thought I was going crazy, and I thought you thought—oh never mind. It's a Luck."

"A Luck?"

"That's what he told me. Like a brownie *and* like a boggart."

Glosson leaned back against the wall. "What the hell is going on? Is this why the cat has been staying off the floor?"

"He belonged to Owen; he lived in that little treasure chest. He was supposed to be for both of us. He's attached himself to just me. I thought I was losing my mind, but you saw him, you heard him. He's real."

"Why didn't you tell me all this?"

"At first it was just dreams, then he started telling me things in the dreams and they happened. I thought I was going crazy and seeing things and I was too scared. I tried to tell you a few times, but I couldn't. I'm telling you now."

10

Cameron shrugged and reach out to squeeze Glosson's knee. "Cats can always see them in the stories. The Luck said that's why Lord Donalbain was acting crazy. It—he said not to call him it—he told me he was the family Luck."

"He belonged to Owen."

Cameron nodded.

The rational world had never really existed. They both had seen and heard the creature. "So what do we do? It's driving us crazy. It's—"

"*He.* Trying to kill you. Sort of. He wants something."

"He wants you?"

"He wants something from both of us."

Glosson heard dishes falling and breaking in the kitchen just as the lights blinked on, off, then stayed off. The night's shadows rushed into the house, eating what light remained. Glosson reached for Cameron's hand, groped, found it, and then he was touching the floor, touching the cat who had appeared from somewhere.

"Cam? Cameron?" Glosson desperately felt around on the floor, the wall, the top of the stairs. "Cameron?"

Thin, high laughter.

The lights came back on. There was the little treasure chest, now locked, a few feet away and no Cameron.

"Cameron! Where are you? Cameron!"

Glosson searched the house, even though he knew it was futile. Upstairs, downstairs, in closets and cabinets, out to the toolshed and everywhere the thin, high laughter followed him. He found himself back upstairs on the landing where Lord Donalbain sat by the treasure chest, a Sphinx on guard.

"What do you want? Please, tell me what you want."

No answer.

Glosson ran to his computer. He didn't find much on Lucks as creatures in folklore, unless Lucks were leprechauns, but they were Irish. If this Luck was like both a brownie and a boggart, then, as brownie, it was a good spirit or a little house god. As boggart, mischief-maker, poltergeist, or a curse. A brownie for Cam, the boggart, his. To get rid of boggarts, leave the house, stay away. But how could he when Cameron was a prisoner in that little chest? Sing off key, hang bells on doors. No bells in the house, just wind chimes which he jingled over and over. A rousing chorus of *auld lang syne* off key, no response. It—*He*— had wanted oatmeal, maybe food was the answer. Brownies, boggarts—he scribbled down the foods to try: porridge and cream, oatcakes. Good Scotch.

An hour later, Glosson was back from the ABC store, Harris Teeter, and the World Market, the latter for imported oatcakes and Flahavan's Irish Oatmeal mix, which Google said was porridge. Then, from the food the Macnabs had left, he grabbed Scottish shortbread and two cans of soup, Baxter's Cullen Skink Cream of Smoked Haddock Soup and Baxter's Cock-a-Leekie Soup. He hoped the oatcakes would go with the soups.

Glosson scooped up his lordship and went half way down the stairs. "All right, Luck. Here are your favorite foods. Please, let me have my husband back. I love him. He's mine; I'm his."

Thin, high laughter.

"We'll go downstairs, let you eat, okay?"

Silence.

He unfolded the futon in the living room part of the downstairs great room and lay down, with Lord Donalbain curled up against him. He left on the light in the stairwell and the floor lamp by the futon. The house was quiet.

Glosson sat up a couple hours later and swung his legs to the floor. "I should go check." Lord Donalbain butted him in the side. He looked down, the cat was staring at him. It climbed into his lap, a weight holding him down. He tried to get up and the cat pressed his head into his chest.

"Are you trying to tell me something?" The cat touched his face.

"All right, all right, I'll stay down here."

He slept on the futon, with Lord Donalbain now by his head.

He dreamed of Cameron, inside the little treasure chest, trying to get out… Glosson had to do what the Luck asked. He had to, he had to, he had to….

Early next morning, in the grey light at dawn, after feeding the cat and then himself, Glosson went back upstairs, carrying more food. Lord Donalbain followed close at his heels. What he had left the night before was gone, the plates stacked, the silverware on top. The treasure chest had not been moved. He set the plates down on the blanket: a jigger of Scotch, and porridge and cream, and a mug of what seemed to be like hot chocolate. He had found a can of something called Ovaltine in the Macnabs' food. It turned out to be like Nesquik.

"Luck, I fed you and I feed you again. Please, let me have my husband back. I love him; he loves me. He's mine; I'm his. You can't have him. What do you want?"

He heard a long sigh, then a gravelly whisper in his head. A long pause, and the words were repeated, but he didn't recognize the language.

"I don't understand," Glosson whispered back. He felt a weight against his leg and looked down to see Lord Donalbain pressing against him. Then, the whisper again: *Take me home.*

Another long pause, and the whisper: *There I will let him go, if he wants to. He has to choose.*

Greensboro to Atlanta to London, *eight, long, long hours, checking again and again to be sure the little chest was in his carry-on … Faerie, the Otherworld, a paradise, eternal summer, eternal happiness…*

A longer day in London,

No sickness or old age or death, take the white ship to the true West…

13

Then a 9:15 p.m. train out of Euston Station, the Caledonian Sleeper, a fitful sleep in a narrow bed, to Perth.

Islands of the Blest, Tir naÓg, Avalon… into the hollow hills, into brilliant flowers, wild woods, emerald mountains, the air heady with perfume…

Asking directions twice to get to Scott Street and Stop U and Bus 15. Another bus in Crieff, the 890 to Killin, arriving 7:40 a.m.

What if he chooses to stay? What will I do? I'll do anything, anything, to have Cameron back.

"You could walk it, sir, to the Killin Hotel," the taxi driver said, laughing, as Glosson fell into the back seat. The man was right, it wasn't far, but even the thought of figuring one more thing out, asking for more directions, was just too much.

He made himself drink tea and eat eggs and toast in the hotel restaurant, with its tall windows overlooking the river. The room was filled with light. He had called Elspeth Macnab right before he booked the trip to Scotland, hoping she could tell him something, anything that would help. She was so sorry, she had never meant for this to happen. She'd just wanted them to have some luck. Yes, Glosson had to take the Luck home. There was no other solution. There was no key. Come to Killin, to the Macnab cemetery on Inchbuie, an island in the Falls of Dochert. Anyone could give him directions. Call the Luck out, and he would keep the bargain and set Cameron free. Smash the treasure chest. No, she couldn't go with him.

"Where are they?" he asked. "Here or There?"

"The Luck is bound to the chest, which is both here and there. More than that I don't know."

Glosson had one more question. "The Luck says Cameron has to choose. What if he chooses to stay?"

"Oh, Glosson, that is beyond me. Owen's ancestors should never have kept it bound to them. The Luck is different There, a different shape, and so is time. It passes at a different rate, like in the stories. That's all I know. Come to my house when it's over.."

Glosson walked first to the bridge, promising himself that he and Cameron would take time to look around before going home. The scenery was stunning, the green mountains rising behind the hotel, the river, the loch, the village itself. He had Cameron's passport, but as to how to fake the entry stamp, he had no idea. Maybe Elspeth could help.

Stay with me. Please stay with me, I love you. Again and again, as if the repetition somehow was magical as well.

On the bridge he stood a moment, looking at the falls, the white river around the rocks, feeling the cold spray on his face. Two or three walkers passed without even a casual glance. Glosson found the small iron gate and the stone steps he had been told to look for. The ruins, the enclosed cemetery, all were quiet. All he could hear was the sounds of the falls and his own breathing. Glosson set the treasure chest in a patch of grass not near any grave and he knelt down. "Luck, you are home in your own country. Bring my love back to me. I have kept my half of the bargain."

He waited and then the chest opened. Thin, grey smoke spiraled out and up and then, the Luck stood by the box, looking around and around, his eyes big in wonder. He stroked his face with his long fingers.

"Welcome home You are free," Glosson said, looking down at the creature. "I set you free. Keep your half of the bargain."

The Luck turned back to the little chest and picked it up and turned it upside down and shook it. At first, Glosson saw only a larger spiral of grey smoke pouring slowly out, making a small cloud on the grass. Light flickered, and Cameron lay there naked, groaning. The Luck stood to one side and Glosson on the other, both watching Cameron. He sat up and looked first at the Luck and then at Glosson. "What? Where are we?"

"Choose," Glosson whispered, choking back the rest of his words, *I love you, please stay, please, please, please stay.* The Luck nodded, and Glosson picked up the chest and smashed

15

it against a rock. He stomped on it to be sure.

The Luck held out his hand. Glosson held out his. Cameron looked again at them both, first, the Luck, second, Glosson.

Cameron took Glosson's hand. Crying, Glosson pulled Cameron up and against him, murmuring, "it's all right, it's over, it's me, it's all right. Here, put this on, I have more back in the hotel. You're in Scotland. He captured you, the Luck, and I had to bring him here. Now we can go home, get his lordship from the vet, whatever you want."

"Yes, yes," Cameron whispered, his face against Glosson's chest.

The Luck floated up and Cameron turned his head to face him. The Luck extended his six-fingered hand and blew towards Cameron. Glosson waited for the heart, like before. Instead, he smelled a faint scent of distant flowers. He watched as Cameron breathed it in, and sighed it out, shuddering against Glosson's chest. Some day he would ask Cameron where he had been.

The Luck dissolved into a grey cloud that twisted away, over the gravestones and out over the white waters of the falls, and into the mists.

Glosson tried not to see the longing in Cameron's face.

Doubting Thomas

Stephen Blake

"For the purposes of the tape, could you state your name please?" Detective Inspector Thomas paused for an answer.

"Please note that the interviewee has declined to give his name." He looked up to the clock on the wall. "It's three thirty p.m. on the 4th February 1988."

Opposite D.I. Thomas, in the police interview room, sat a small figure of a man. His face was badly pitted. His nose, cheeks and chin, all red and shiny, seemed too large for his face. His permanent toothy grin did little to improve his features. Thomas looked him up and down. He didn't have far to look, as the man was impossibly short. Most would assume it was dwarfism. D.I. Thomas never assumed a thing.

He'd been put onto the case about abducted children for a specific reason. He was the most thorough officer the force had. His colleagues called him 'Doubting Thomas.' He never believed or assumed anything until he could categorically prove it. The Crown Prosecution Service loved him. Every case was presented to them gift wrapped.

In this case, children had been taken from various places. Mostly from their homes, and always returned within twenty-four hours. Many returned ecstatically happy, some trembling and traumatised. They were toddlers, barely able to speak, let alone explain what had happened. There were no clues as to how, who, or even why.

After months of abductions, parents in uproar, and MP's questioning the ability of the police, D.I. Gareth Thomas had been called in. He'd already been the one to link numerous cases, to see the thread, the similarities. The more publicity, the more parents came forward to say it had happened to them – *they thought*. Few were positive, given how quickly the children returned. Some reports had to be dismissed as parents covering up for leaving the kids alone.

The case was really bothering him. There was no sign of a forced entry, nothing to suggest a struggle, and when the kids came back, again no sign or evidence to suggest who was behind this. The papers were full of panic-mongers, suggesting an international paedophile ring was behind it all. It all meant more and more pressure for answers.

And then, this man had walked into the station. He'd demanded to talk to Thomas and no one else. He had information about the abductions. The police were so desperate they spoke to all the crackpots confessing to it. They had to. They had no lines of enquiry, no leads – nothing.

"So, Sir, you have information for us regarding the abduction of numerous children over the last few months. Is that correct?"

The grinning man bobbed his head in a nod.

"Do you think you could elaborate for me? Perhaps start at the beginning?"

Again, he bobbed his head. He took in a long breath, and when he spoke, his voice danced over the words. "The beginning you say? Ooh that's a long way back."

He might as well have said 'Tra-la-lah-la-lah' because when he spoke, that's how it sounded.

Thomas composed himself. "Sir, I have no problem with your anonymity, but what I must insist on are facts. Can you give me any, at all?"

Still grinning, he replied, "Why, of course. The beginning you say. Well, we fairy folk..."

"Don't waste my time with this bullshit! Either tell me the truth or piss off!" Thomas had seen three crackpots already today, and his patience was wearing thin.

The grin never faltered, the man simply said, "Claire Louise Jones – 21 North Parade. Toby Daniels – 13 Wisley Drive. Joanne Hall – 5 Redcliffe Way. Shall I go on?"

Thomas shifted forward in his chair. "You've got my attention. None of those names have been given to the press. So, are you a part of this, or a witness?"

The grin had an air of smugness about it now. "As I was saying, we fairy folk have long lived with you humans. For some time now, we've had a problem. The closest thing I can compare it to for you to understand is global warming. You know, the majority agree it exists and it's a problem, and then, nothing. People wait for someone to just fix it. Some take some minor steps to correct things, whilst the rest look on. And some sit to one side, in denial that there even is a problem." He blinked for a moment and tilted his head. "Are you with me so far?"

Thomas was grinding his teeth. "Yeah, I'm following you just fine. Can we bring everything up to date? How about up to where the abducted children come into it?" He shook his head in disbelief, wondering why he was even tolerating listening to this loon. *The children, that's why,* he thought. He composed himself. "Please, continue."

"Very well, Gareth."

Thomas shot him a look. *How does he know my name?* He kept that thought to himself and let the little man continue.

"Our problem was our magic, it..."

Thomas stood up from his chair. "Look, if you are not prepared to talk to me properly, I'm going to lock you up until a police appointed psychiatrist can assess you and then we'll talk again. Right now, you're wasting my time."

He moved to leave the room but remembered the tape. "Interview suspended at sixteen hundred hours..."

"Bethany Megan Thomas – 17 St Clements Street."

Thomas' hand was hovering over the stop button of the tape machine. He stared hard at the little man. His hovering hand began to shake. He drew his hands in, folding his arms, holding his anger in. When he spoke, he did so with great care over each word so as to not give in to the rage growing within. "My daughter? What about her?"

He raised his hand to the man, stopping him from replying. He fumbled in his jacket on the back of the chair. Finding his mobile telephone, he dialled his home number. "Roz, it's me. Where is Beth? Are you sure? Make sure. Yeah, I'll hang on."

He looked at the impish man, still smiling, still grinning ear to ear.

"You're sure? Calm down. Roz! Calm down! She'll be back, and soon. No, just stay calm. I'm dealing with it. I don't have time to argue with you about my tone. Just hang on there and I'll sort it out here. Look, I'm hanging up. She

20

will be fine." He was speaking to his wife harshly, he knew. Now, more tenderly, he said, "I won't let anything bad happen to her. I will get her back. I promise." He hung up and carefully sat down. It was taking all his years of experience to hold back the tidal wave of anger, fear and desperation he was feeling. Through gritted teeth, he spoke. "What do you want? What do I have to do to get her back?"

The small man broke into something akin to a happy clap. "You just need to let me finish my story. When we're done here, little Bethany will be with her mother once more.

"Now then, where did I get to? Oh yes, magic. You see, we get magic from humans really. Your belief in us gives us power. It works rather like a superstition or a curse. The more you believe in it, the more powerful it becomes. So we came up with a plan. We thought why not let the humans see us more. Do you remember those two little naughty girls who pretended to take pictures with us?"

Thomas nodded. Of course he'd read about the 'Cottingley Fairies.' Two girls had fooled Sir Arthur Conan Doyle, creator of Sherlock Holmes, that they had genuine photographic evidence of fairies.

"Well, for a short while then, we all noticed an immense increase in our abilities. I am not ashamed to tell you that many found it quite addictive, and they were not happy to see it wane as people came to realise the pictures were faked. There is a fine line between getting masses to believe, and the same masses thinking it is all a hoax."

Thomas saw an opportunity to take a different tack with the man. "So were they fake or did your people pose for them?"

"We were there, watching Frances and Elsie with their little cut out pictures. But no, none are real. You can see for yourself that I am not, by human standards, a pretty thing. We do laugh at how you all think we look. I've seen that

Tinkerbell. If only! Hah, I've never seen one of ours look that good, or come to think of it, have a dress that short." He slapped his thigh, laughing loudly to himself.

Thomas turned away from the table, running his fingers through his hair, slowing his breathing, trying to keep a grip on reality. He knew in his mind that the small man was just deluded. He composed himself once more, knowing he had to do this right, for the sake of his daughter and every other child that had been taken. He turned around to the little man.

"What the hell are you doing?" Thomas was disgusted to see him with one hand down his trousers, cooing the name 'Tinkerbell' over and over.

"Sorry lad, she really gets me going. Why, I was only telling a little girl, the same age as your Bethany, just the other day, about..."

Thomas knocked the man off the chair and carried him by his neck to the opposite wall. Holding him by his throat, so that his small legs dangled beneath him, he pressed hard to choke him and then let him drop to the floor.

He stepped back from the prone man and looked to the door. He expected someone to run in and tell him to stop the interview now. He expected to be suspended, maybe even disciplinary action, but the door did not open. No one came in.

The man brushed himself down as he stood and looked at Thomas.

"Now then, Gareth, this is not you. This is not 'Doubting' Thomas, the man who is always in control. Emotion set aside, just a seeker of truth. Get a grip, lad, and not on my neck."

Thomas fiddled with his tie. "Look, what do you want? Just tell me, so that I can have my little girl home," he pleaded.

"Right, where did we get to with my tale?" He pushed the chair up on its legs again and climbed onto the seat. "Ah, yes, we got to the fact that we get our magic from you humans, and that a lot of my people have, well, gone cold turkey."

"Bethany... What about my daughter!? Is she safe!?"

"I'm getting to it. She's fine. You see, we've done lots of nice things for you lot over the years. In fact, even you will agree, most of the children come back to the parents happy. Happiest they've been for years for some of them." He scratched the side of his head. "I got to thinking about how believing in something works, and I wondered if fearing something might work better than just believing or happy memories."

Thomas took his seat opposite him again. "Just say, I go along with this nonsense you are spouting. Believing and fearing are not the same things. You can fear the 'Boogeyman' but you might not necessarily believe in him. Children might fear the monster in the closet or under the bed. That fear is forgotten over time. And did they ever actually believe?"

"Ah, you have a point. No, I've not explained it properly. We've always let children see us. Unlike any monster under the bed, we are very real. Kids believe, and then as they grow, that belief diminishes, and with it, our power. Now, scare a child, really frighten them - touch them, so they know how real we are." He licked his lips hungrily. "Now that stays with them to the grave." His deep set eyes twinkled. Thomas got the distinct impression that this man was one of those who frightened children, and he seemed like he enjoyed his work.

"You said you would not hurt Bethany!"

"I said she's fine. Bit of counselling... ah, never mind that. She's with a good crowd who just like playing games. They won't hurt her, unless... well, our conversation is going nicely, so it won't come to that." He rocked to himself, seemingly enjoying this phase of the conversation.

He clicked his fingers and then looked at them for a while. "Hmm, it's getting there. Starting to feel it," he pondered to himself.

"Feel what?"

"Don't you worry yourself about that, Gareth. You've been very attentive and patient. I'm going to reward you for that. How would you like to go and collect Bethany?"

"Now? Really? Of course I do. Let's go."

"Well, why don't we go in your car? I've always wanted to go in one of them."

Thomas didn't need to be asked twice. He stopped the tape and went to the door, before returning to the tape recorder and ejecting the tape. He popped it into his pocket and motioned for the man to follow him.

The station bustled as usual but no one paid either of them any attention. Thomas turned to the man. "Can they not see you?"

"Oh, I like the way you are thinking. We may well be getting close to the end now, Gareth." He snapped his fingers again, and this time a small, blue spark appeared. "Not long now."

Thomas rubbed his eyes and, after retrieving his car keys, headed toward the parking area. His mind was in turmoil. The things he was seeing. The things he'd heard said. His usually calm and ordered mind was frantically searching for obvious answers. The one he settled on was that this was a man suffering from dwarfism, failed plastic surgery, and had come from a travelling circus where he had a magic act. He rubbed the back of his neck. Logic was not helping here.

After a lot of messing around, they were in the car, hopefully heading to Bethany. The messing around had been the passenger's insistence on a booster cushion for the front seat so that he could see clearly as they drove along.

His face pressed to the window of the car door. His putrid breath steamed the glass as he turned his stumpy, gnarled hands over and over in his lap. Taking in every view, he became excitable, making grunting noises toward the people they passed. Toward the children they passed.

They cruised by a playground. The strange man became jittery, excited. Thomas looked across at him to see drool running down his chin. The idea of this 'man' being anywhere near his daughter filled him with a deep terror. He had read all of the paedophile profiles, watched the disgusting videos and seen the vile photographs. He'd worried he had become desensitised to it all. Now, though, it was his own child, his only daughter, and he deeply wished he'd never seen those things. He desperately wanted to be ignorant of the cruel horror these repulsive creatures did.

He shook his head, trying to clear the images. All those images, they all appeared in his mind with Bethany's face, with her eyes looking straight at him. He physically shuddered. His policeman's training worked its way forward, working out how to engage with his passenger.

He cleared his throat with a cough and said, "So, fear is the name of the game for you now then?" He decided to keep him talking, try to get him to reveal some more information.

"Well, let's say it is an experiment. A little bit of a test."

"Is my daughter, is she, is she a part of this test?" The words got caught in his throat as his emotions threatened to overcome him.

"Now, Gareth, I told you young Bethany was all right and I meant it. No, I've put forward another idea to the elders."

He shuffled in his seat, distracted, as he attempted to take in every sight outside the car window.

"And the other idea is?"

"It's a very good one in my opinion. Third house on the right is yours I believe."

"The idea?"

"That recording you have in your pocket. It won't work by the way. Our chat is a private one." He winked at Thomas.

Pulling the tape from his pocket, he pushed it into the cassette player in his car. Silence, and then a voice, giggling. He recognised it immediately. It was Bethany. Tears rolled over his cheeks.

"How about we give you back your little one, at least for now?"

Thomas' heart leapt. He undid his seat belt and pulled the door handle. A click of the man's stubby fingers, a flash of blue light, and the door would not open. He pulled hard at the handle. He rammed his shoulder into it. He tried the window. He climbed into the back of the car and tried both rear doors without success.

Eyes red with tears, he begged, "Let me see her, please!"

"Gareth, my boy, calm yourself." His voice was cold. The grin remained but a serious tone settled on each of his words. "You, a man of logic, a man of facts, do believe that I can take your daughter from you whenever I so choose?"

Thomas, now on the back seat, threw himself toward the man. He pushed and punched the air but was unable to move.

"Hmmm, yes, I can feel that you do. Well, this is nice. I cannot describe the feeling to you. It just makes the air fizzle. I want you to hold onto what you are feeling right now. I want you to know that I can, and will, take young Bethany anytime I feel like it. Maybe she could dress up as 'Tinkerbell' for my visits?"

Exhausted, physically and emotionally, Thomas whispered, "What do you want?"

"That's my boy. Well, firstly, look over there."

Through the window at the front of the house, Thomas saw his wife embracing their daughter, both of them crying and smiling.

"See, I told you she would be fine. Now, as to what I want? For this to never ever happen to your family again? It's simple, really, Detective Inspector 'Doubting' Thomas."

He fixed him with an intense stare. Another click of the fingers, a burst of bright blue light, and he vanished.

Thomas sagged. Sweat beaded on his forehead. He reached for the door handle but it would still not open. He flopped back on the rear seat.

Breathing heavily, his mind whirred. The light disappeared from within the car, sucked away, leaving only pitch black. His eyes could not penetrate the void. Within the dark vacuum, his ears only heard the thudding of his heart.

Without warning, two stumpy hands reached from behind him, grabbing hold of his neck. He was unable to move, frozen in position. Close to his ear, the man's voice whispered, "Believe. That's all you have to do. Believe."

OBSESSION

Angel Blackwood

Ulfer paced before the mirror, glancing at the black glass on each pass. He gave a snorting huff and stopped in front of it, taking the few steps forward to glare at himself. He slid clawed fingers through his long hair and watched the inky strands slide across his cracked, black skin. He sneered at himself, and his white eyes flared. The cracks running through his flesh slowly glowed to life like a river lit by the moon. He shook his head and ran his fingertip over one.

With a groan, Ulfer twisted away from the mirror and grabbed his horns, tugging sharply. If he could only get the woman out of his mind. He jerked again and hissed as pain shot down the sides of his neck. He stole a glance over his shoulder and bit his lip. After a moment's consideration, he spun back to the mirror and narrowed his eyes on the black glass. Just a glance. Just one.

He breathed deeply, focusing his power on an image of her. Black feathers cascading down around her pale, narrow face. The light shining along the same black feathers that fanned out from her arms. Glinting in her golden-brown eyes. The little musical chirrup she gave when he kissed the base of her neck. He shuddered as the image in the mirror swirled into focus. She kneeled in her garden, the early morning light shimmering from the sleek feathers. He gave a little sigh and touched the image with trembling fingers.

He let out a quivering breath and swiped his fingers over his face and up to his horn, tugging fiercely as she dug in the dirt. He groaned and gave his head a fierce shake. The glow flared brightly, and he growled as he pushed the image away. Just one glance. That's what he'd said and that's what he meant. If he didn't end it now, he'd spend all day staring at her. He had some sort of meeting with Haakon. The commander would not be kept waiting.

Ulfer gave a little sigh and brushed his fingers down the glass again before whipping the black cloth over it. He got halfway across the room before the pull of the mirror stopped him. He hesitated there, shifting from foot to foot. He tugged at his horn again and forced himself to turn back to the door. He slipped out into the hall and slammed the door. With a little shudder, he started off, trailing his fingers over the twisted roots and vines that made up the walls.

The firefly lights flitted across the roof as he walked, but he paid them no heed. Her golden eyes sparked across his vision, and he twitched, swatting at the air in front of his face. He snarled and shook his head. When that didn't work, he briefly closed his eyes and tried to force the image from his mind. Her eyes were replaced by a breathy sigh and the sun shimmering along her porcelain breasts as they heaved beneath him.

His eyes shot open. He paused just outside Haakon's door and lifted his fingertips to his face. With only a brief hesitation, he struck himself as hard as he could. The fireflies swirled in agitation above him, but they didn't matter. What mattered was that the image was gone. He took a few steadying breaths before giving a series of curt knocks. A muffled "come in" came to him through the door, and he pushed it open.

Haakon reclined in a moss-green chair, his pale, pastel purple skin seeming sickly next to the green. He smiled and indicated the chair beside him. Ulfer slipped inside and closed the door. The glowing crystals embedded in the walls flared brighter at a flick of Haakon's fingers. Ulfer walked over and sat in the chair, folding his hands over his lap. Haakon shifted forward and rested his arms on his knees, the pale light glinting in his hard, plum eyes.

"I'm concerned, Ulfer."

"What about?"

"The guards near the portal, they've reported to me that you've been going into the mortal world more and more frequently. Can you tell me why?" He shifted and a wave of hair so dark violet it looked like ink slid across his shoulder, and Ulfer couldn't help but imagine her inky feathers sliding over her shoulder the same way.

His hands trembled, and he clasped them tighter. "I've been going over in search of the half-fae. I was instructed to bring them here by any means necessary. I'm to hunt them."

"You aren't hunting them." He slid his hand under his leg and produced one shadow black feather. "Alakest says he saw you with one of the bird women. Is that true?"

"Yes, master, but only because –"

"You know it's forbidden to speak with those filthy creatures. Birds." He sneered and spat on the mossy floor. "Vermin."

He leaned forward and stabbed one lavender finger against Ulfer's chest. "Forbidden to speak with them. You do things with this woman that makes the bile rise." He shook his head, his eyes sparkling dangerously. "Never again."

Ulfer closed his eyes, the images of her dancing through his mind. He gave a little groan but nodded. Haakon smiled and leaned back in his seat.

"Very good. Now, go to the portal and relieve Mefaly."

"Of course." He gave a bow of his head and rose, hurrying to the door.

When he was back in the hall, the firefly lights flickered on and flitted over his head as he rushed to the portal. He shooed Mefaly away and took his place. It was a matter of moments before he was drumming his fingertips behind him against the wall. He glanced at the stretch of vines beside him, wishing desperately to step through and run to his woman. His beautiful, forbidden bird.

The other guard glanced over, rainbow spiral eyes flicking nervously over his body and taking in the drumming fingers, the sheen of sweat. Ulfer narrowed his white eyes and bared his fangs. The man turned quickly to the front. Ulfer slid his fingers along the wall and groaned. He was so close. So close. His body shuddered, and he closed his eyes. He needed to go to her. One more time. She deserved to know what Haakon said. Once more and never again.

His tongue darted across his lips. He swayed a bit, images of Haakon and his beloved jumbled together until all he could do was whine in one long, uninterrupted note. The words "never again" and her breathy sighs filled his head until, with a snarl, he pushed away from the wall and shot through the portal. Just once more. Then never again.

F AIRY D REAMS

Layne Calry

Chapter One

Mammet stood staring into the glistening pool that sat near her window. She ran her fingers along the seam of her dress. She shifted. Uneasy. An anxious air to her mind. Her long, blonde hair shimmered in the iridescent moonbeams that shined down. She sighed, kneeled, and dipped a finger in the water to watch it ripple and move about. Marveling at the wrinkles as they went from small to large and then disappeared. It appeared so calm, but even the smallest thing could cause a disturbance.

Her gaze caught the black rot that lay on the ground. Only a few inches of discolored earth, but enough to bring tears to her eyes. She touched it with gentle fingers, rubbed as if to remove it. However, when pale fingers were lifted back to her, the dark spot still lay there, like death.

We are all dying. All of us. We have been dying for centuries. As people have started to forget about us. Have moved on from us. I want to know what love is again. I want to love someone without condition. Nabiuma, of course, but I want more. More before I pass into oblivion. Surely they can grant me such a request.

A noise behind her had her turning her purple gaze to the man that stood in the shadows. Dark skinned with eyes of deepest green settled upon her. He was beautiful, and he was hers, but she found no enjoyment in his presence on this night. She frowned and looked away.

She whispered to him, "Nabiuma, it is silent here these long years. Won't you let me find a little one to fill our halls with laughter? Like centuries before? Something to love just for a little while."

Nabiuma looked at her and shook his head. "My dearest love, you know the rules. The council has long ago forbade us. We dare not take the human children. Even if they may save us. Or bring happiness. What of an animal? Another tree like your grand willow?"

Mammet stared at him, tears winking in her eyes. She shook her head. "No, Nabi. I want a child, a human child. Something to hold and sing to and play. A tree is beautiful and alive, but it is not the same, neither are animals."

Mammet moved, the barest of rustling coming from her back from the white fairy wings that adorned her with golden swirls. She sighed and brushed at her eyes. Nabiuma moved forward and placed a hand on her shoulder and then lay his arm around her, pulling her close to his side.

"My dear Mammet. I am sorry. I know how much you want children. I do too, but even our impending deaths cannot force our hand. We cannot capture a child."

She sighed and shifted. "I said nothing of capturing. You make it sound so dire and evil."

Mammet shrugged his arm off and touched the petal of the flower nearest her, kneeling by the pond. She traced its shape, muttering under her breath as it began to change its color to turn a bright purple. Then suddenly she gasped and looked up.

"It is against the rules to steal the children. Something I would not do anyway. I am not cruel. As the humans started to hunt our kind, we stopped allowing them entry, but what if the child comes willingly? And what if they can save us? We need them to believe again. And Nabi, I want a little of that happiness before I am gone. So many others experienced it. I did not."

Nabiuma shook his head. "Mammet."

She waved her hands. "No, do not patronize me. A child can make choices, and we could keep them happy once they came. And the baby, it would forget after time. So why wouldn't it work? I want to hear children's laughter again, Nabi. I want to hear them playing and dancing and singing. I want to view their happiness as they grow and prosper. Their innocence is refreshing. I want that again before I am gone. I have never had one of my own, only glimpsed the small ones through the centuries. Just one child, Nabi."

Nabiuma scoffed and stared at her and spoke. "And what is to happen once the child begins to age? What then, my love? You will care for them as they age and die? It will be heartbreaking. We are dying. Yes, my love, but we still have much more time than a human lifespan. And children will not save us; it will not even save you. It is just something that you want before you are gone."

Mammet bit her lip and smoothed out the front of her dress. "No. I will only keep them until they are eighteen, and then, then I will allow them to return to the human world. With the gifts they learn here, they will prosper in the human world."

Mammet spun away, her eyes flashing. "Yes, Nabiuma, it seems selfish. But how can it be if I am willing to allow them to leave?"

Nabiuma stared at her and shook his head. He moved forward and grasped her arms, holding onto her with loose fingers.

"My dearest Mammet, the child will be different. It will not be able to speak of us, and what of their real parents? The parents that you steal them from? What then, love? Do you really want to cause such harm? Out there in the world, Mammet, it is different. People do not believe in us anymore. What will happen to a child when they go and speak of us? They act cruelly now, the humans. Yes. They used to murder, maim. But now they do with silence. They harm the mind in ways that we cannot even fathom. Why subject a child to that? Why mark them bizarre in an unforgiving world?"

Mammet shifted again. "There are children that no one wants, Nabi. I have seen them, heard their cries. And many of them turn into animals. Hurt, sad animals. Please. The child will say nothing. A little piece of happiness for it and for me?"

Nabiuma sighed and ran his hands across his face. He met his beloved's eyes. Mammet brushed at them.

"Oh Mammet. Your dreams are always so full of happiness and want. But, my dearest, you must think of consequences and such things. Yes, you would give them a small piece of happiness. Yes, they buy us a little bit of life, but what about when you have to let them go? You will be casting them out just as their original families did. You will break them all over again."

Mammet's lower lip trembled, and she blinked in quick succession. Pulling away from him, she moved away.

"Leave me, Nabiuma, please. I want to be alone."

"Mammet." He stepped closer, and she shook her heard furiously.

"I said leave me!"

36

Nabiuma let his hands drop to his sides, and he looked back at her with a saddened gaze. "Very well, my love. I will come back to check on you."

Mammet nodded, crossing her arms. Once he was out of ear shot, she settled to the ground and curled her arms around her legs and let the tears flow like rain. Great hiccoughing sobs wracked her body, and she brushed again and again at her wet cheeks, but there was nothing to stem the flow.

There was an emptiness to her barrenness. A sadness that she could not shake. Her want for children was growing large and overtaking every part of her mind and soul. It had been for years, but now even more so as her life was ending. She wished to end it happy.

I do not wish to harm them. I do not wish to make them sad or break them. What if I can go to the human realm? Even for a bit. I will bring just one child, just one before my demise. One who chooses to come. I will care for them.

As the tears began to cease, she wiped at her eyes one last time, and her purple gaze took in the surrounding area. She trailed her fingers along the pond, and with a soft sigh, she stood. Clenching her fists, she nodded to her reflection.

"I will make my dreams come true. This place must see a child again. I must see a child again. It has been far too long since a fairy carried a child or a human child passed into this realm, but not anymore. We all need that happiness."

Mammet hurried away, the whispering of her gown all that was heard on the moon-filled air. She would have her dreams; she would have children again. She just needed to find a way to make it so.

Mammet paced back and forth, the ground beneath her leaving a trail of footprints in the muddy earth. At the first barest whisper of doors, she hurried to it and stared into the brown eyes of Nabiuma. Her heart fell at the weariness she saw there, the way his shoulders dropped. He held out his hand and began to speak, but Mammet shook her head.

"The council has refused both of my requests, haven't they?"

Nabiuma sighed and nodded his head. "I am sorry, my dear. I did try, but they said it would be unsafe for the fae to travel between worlds, even to sway a child who has no home to come back. And the more we gather and then send back, the more we risk exposure to our world. I am sorry. Even one child would cause undue tension, and they do not wish to allow you to go to the human realm. Even just for the years it would take you to procure and raise a child. The exposure to our world would be too great. There are no guardians anymore."

Mammet pushed a hand to her mouth, biting at her knuckles with tears streaming down her face, to quiet the wails that wished to break free.

"Only one child for a lifetime. How would the humans put it together? It would be a missing child that no one cares about but me. Why can't it be like before! When we could just bring the children here or visit them there? And if not that, why can they not let me leave for the seventy years to see a lifetime. A lifetime that is a mere minute to us? I would tell no one. I would not need a guardian."

Nabiuma sighed and shook his head, his own eyes wet. "I am sorry, Mammet. There are policies now and politics. We are a dying race. Too much magic, and humans, they always want magic. And without permission, if you go out there, you will lose it faster than if you went with permission. I am sorry, love. And there is no guarantee that your magic would stay intact for that seventy years. We must protect our race."

Mammet turned her gaze to the ground, fisting her hands, pushing them into her stomach. Great, hiccoughing gasps began to shake her.

Nabiuma reached forward, and Mammet stepped back.

"Do not speak to me of a dying race. We are dying. We will be dead, and they cannot grant me one small request? One small thing. You talk of saving our race. What is to save, Nabi! We are all broken, sad creatures. There is nothing left of the once proud fairy folk. Even our wings have become translucent. I can barely see yours. They were beautiful once, black and gold. One thing, Nabi, just one thing so I could die happy."

She turned and ran from him, mud splashing on her ivory legs. She cried out as her dress snagged, and she tugged it free, tears sliding from her eyes. She found the great willow. The tree she loved so much, the tree she had nurtured from a seed. Watched it grow tall and beautiful. She kneeled at the side. She leaned against its trunk, feeling the rough bark between her fingers as she gripped it tight.

"I only ask for one, one little one to love for eighteen years. It cannot be that bad. They say I risk exposure to the worlds, of our own world. But why do I stay somewhere where I am not happy. We are dying anyway, so what is the risk to our race? There are only a few handful of the old ones and a hundred strong of the young ones."

She gave a shuddering breath and crossed her arms, holding her elbows with the palms of her hands.

There was a time when children and adults begged to come here. Begged to be part of our homes. People gave us their children when they could not care for them. Now we are nothing but forgotten. Our magic is fading. More and more of our kind have drifted onward and away, some even to the human realm to never return. I would do that if I didn't need permission. They would never give it to me now, fearful that I would lose my mind and bring a child back, but perhaps… Perhaps it is time to stop caring what they think? To steal the happiness for myself. Perhaps the mortals have it right. And we are not the superior race, as our people would have us believe.

Mammet wiped at her eyes and took a sharp breath, holding her hands folded across her heart. She shifted, listening to Nabiuma's voice as it bounced around the trees. It resounded and echoed, making her shudder. Tugging at her broken heart.

Mammet heard him calling to her, begging her to come to him. She looked around. It was only a matter of time before her Nabiuma found her. She must act now. Throwing caution to the wind, she stood. She ran, long legs tearing up the ground as she made it breathless to their haven, their home. Tossing what she could into a bag, she quickly wrote him a small letter. She gave one last look around and then turned before she could talk herself out of leaving the letter and the realm.

My dearest Nabi,

Though I wish that I could find it in my heart to stay, I cannot. There is too much sadness that weighs heavy on me. I am not happy nor carefree as I once was. I am not the pretty fae that you fell in love with. Something is missing, and there is a chunk that does not fit here in this world. So, I will be leaving; to the human realm I will go. Do not worry. I will be fine, and if you should find it in your heart to follow, my dearest, look for the Lily of the Valley that grows to the sky.

Love,

Mammet

Mammet brushed at her eyes as she laid the white paper on their oak table. Covering her mouth, she hurried away before her love for her mate would force her to stay where she was unhappy. She, however, could not bear to make Nabiuma come, not when he was happy where he was. She could hold onto the hope that he would chose to follow on his own. Her dear Nabiuma was loyal to a fault, to her, to his race, but his people always won out over her. And that was as a good fairy should be.

Perhaps I am not, nor have I ever been, a good fairy.

Mammet hurried to the door that blocked their realms, the deep red of its color burning her eyes. She touched its smooth edges, feeling the pulsing beneath her hand. She watched in awe as glowing letters began to burn into the door's face. She traced them with her fingers, eying them. Choosing the correct ones, the secret to open the door.

She looked once behind her. She knew that if she went through the door, she could not come back. No fairy left the fae plain without permission. Especially now that no human guardian would be there to save them. And if they did, they were no longer welcome in the realm. She was about to break their ultimate rule, and she found she couldn't summon the energy to care.

One last time, her eyes traced the tall trees of the realm. Traced the footpaths of the folk. And for a brief moment, she remembered what it was like centuries ago, and then she let it go. A new life, a new adventure.

She dipped her head at the first wail that rent the silence, the cry of her beloved. She loved him, but her want, no, her need to have something of her own, something she could teach and love and care for, that was even more important than her mate. However, she hoped he would follow her. She would want to share that with him.

She sniffed and pushed with both hands, her wings quivering as she pulled the coat over top of them. Hiding them from view, she would add her magical glamour soon enough. She would need all her magic to pass into the realm. And then, then it would begin to fade faster than it already was. And one day, her wings would even disappear completely.

Mammet stepped into the human realm and gasped at the first sights that assaulted her. There were no trees except the few that stood on either side of her, blocking her from momentary view. She looked down. The grass. It ended as pavement began. Her heart fell at the lack of wildflowers and rivers.

She quivered at the sounds, their overly loud screeching and horn blowing. The low rumble as people spoke and shouted back and forth at each other. She had seen pictures of such things, but to see them in person, it hurt. She reached with her hands to cover her ears, the sensitive buds aching. She blinked, the sun assaulting her eyes as she tried to gather her concentration.

Where do I go from here? What do I do? I can't go back, so I must go forward, but where? There is no human guardian to lead me the way. We have not imparted one on the doors in centuries, and most have died. And those that would be alive, they would not know of us or they would be far too old to keep me safe.

An older man with a twinkle in his eye stepped forward and gazed at the woman. Mammet met his gaze and stared at him with curiosity. She couldn't help the small smile that graced her face. His was a kind countenance. He was so old. There were wrinkles upon wrinkles upon his face, and the aged bronze of his skin had her wondering what color he truly was.

She looked down and shivered. Pulling the coat tighter around herself, she shifted. Mammet adjusted the bag on her shoulder, squeezing the strap with pale fingers. She sniffed and startled as the man spoke. She blinked once and tilted her head.

"Pretty lady? Are you lost? Can I help you find a way home? A fairy ring perhaps, for only a lady such as pretty as you would be a fae."

Mammet gasped and stared at him.

How does he know my secret? Are there guardians left? Surely not? Even Nabiuma says they are all gone. And he would not lie.

She looked to her shoulders to see if her wings peeked out of her coat. The old man wheezed and gave a small chuckle.

"I was only teasing, my dear girl, only teasing. Come along, I know that look well. You look lost. It will not do you well to be lost in such a place as this. Too many girls have that look. There are monsters of men around her. Come along. My wife would have my hide were I not to bring you home. Tell me that I was twenty times a fool."

"Oh really, I am not lost. Please, I am just…"

The old man chuckled and then wheezed once and shook his head. "Now, now dear girl. Are you really not lost? Then why such a dejected look on your face? Let an old man help you out. Do you really want me to get in trouble with my dear wife?"

He blinked up at her, and Mammet couldn't quiet the small giggle that burst forth from her maw. "No, I wouldn't want you to get in trouble."

He chuckled and turned, motioning for her to follow him. He hobbled toward a small ice cream cart. Mammet studied the cart, the white of its surface against the backdrop of blue. The pretty pink ice cream and cone that adorned the side. When the old man reached for the handles, she rushed forward.

"Oh, no, let me help you. I will help. You just lead the way."

She placed her hands along the cool handles. Marveling at the smoothness beneath her hands, and she grunted as she lifted upward. She had not realized it would be so heavy, but she shook her head. She would help him.

The older man smiled and leaned heavily against his cane. "Luck favors me today. Such a pretty maid to help me carry my load. My wife will like you. Such a sweet little thing as you."

She smiled and nodded. *Perhaps I am the lucky one. Nabiuma had spoken of cruelty, but I seem to have found a nice one. And his intentions are pure. I feel it there, the pulsing of him, his essence. It is fading as is my magic, but he is good.*

Mammet followed behind him, taking in all the sights all around them. The fast vehicles of metal and frames. She shuddered at the cool glint of steel as they flew past. The people that walked back and forth, hurriedness dogging their steps.

"Everyone is in such a hurry." She covered her mouth, not realizing until just then she had spoken aloud. The old man turned and smiled.

"I take it you're from a small town, girly? No one has time to slow down anymore. It's just go, go, and go. I tell you, I preferred the simpler times, when people actually held a conversation in your living room and didn't rush off to hurry to nowhere."

Mammet stared at the rushing people and dipped her head, brushing at her eyes. "You could say that I suppose."

The old man touched her shoulder. "Aww now, missy, don't you go crying up a storm. My wife will give me a tongue lashing you won't soon forget if I made you cry."

Mammet giggled at the man's playful glance and nodded her head. "Okay."

"Harry! Harold. Where have you been? You were to be back an hour ago. The kids from the home are down. They want to hear your stories about angels and goodness knows what else you knock around in that head of yours."

"Ah Melanie. I am sorry, my dear. I got caught up." He motioned with his head toward the fairy.

Mammet watched as a plump older woman rushed from what must be the ice cream parlor, her hands upon her robust hips. Mammet covered her mouth at the playful banter between the two, but teared up as she thought of her Nabiuma. Slowly, the older woman realized she was there and toddled forward.

"Now Harry, why didn't you tell me you brought a guest? I tell you, he would lose his head if it weren't attached. Bet he didn't even tell you his name, did he? Well, I am Melanie, and that old codger is Harold, but he goes by Harry. Come inside. You look famished. Nothing but skin and bones. What did you say your name was, my dear girl?"

Mammet smiled and shook her head. "Oh, no I couldn't impose. My name is Mammet." Melanie shook her gray head.

"Oh, nonsense. You look dead on your feet, and I bet you my Harry, he found you in the park. Wouldn't have brought you home if you had a place to stay, am I right? Mammet, what an unusual name. It is an exotic name, that is. So pretty."

Mammet smiled and followed behind the two, pushing their cart. As they stepped into the brisk coolness of the parlor, Mammet's smile grew wider. The children's laughter swirled around her, and she sighed.

Melanie patted the girl's arm and smiled. "That sound does a heart good, does it not? My Harry and me, we've been running this parlor for twenty years. Today is Friday, and the children from the group homes come on down and have a treat."

The old woman sighed and folded her hands into her apron. "Not much else those babies have that gives them joy but the sweet taste of our treats. Now come along. You mind helping? I'll give you some supper and a place to lay your head in return."

Mammet stared at the children as they laughed and shouted at each other. The littlest ones with stickiness on their faces. Mammet was startled out of her thoughts by a small arm grasping her leg and holding on. She smiled and nodded her head, looking up at Melanie, her eyes misty.

"I would love to help."

Melanie smiled and motioned. "Come along then."

This is where I belong.

Mammet smiled at the thought and stepped forward to weave her way through the throng of children.

Chapter Two

Mammet blew a stray hair from her forehead, growling at the large bag of nuts as she wrestled with it.

"Why does he have to get these in bulk?" She mumbled under her breath, anxious to get the toppings out to Harold.

There were children waiting for their snack. Today was Friday, and that meant the kids from the community center came down with their group homes. Today they got a special treat for being good throughout the week. And she loved it. It was beautiful, just as it had been a year ago.

Has it really been that long? I have been here for a year?

Mammet glanced behind her at the empty spot where her wings had been, and she sighed. Only sometimes she missed them. But they were something she had given up readily for a chance at human life, for a chance to raise or be around children.

She smiled to herself. Finally, she got to hear the laughter of little ones and help them with their needs. She could brush their silken curls and smile as they spoke. It was wonderful, and though her heart broke that her Nabiuma was not here to join her, she couldn't help but find contentment in her situation.

Mammet settled the bag at the door, and she leaned against the frame, watching Harold and Melanie as they engaged the children with Harry's stories and Melanie's mouthwatering desserts. It was beautiful to the small fae. She touched her hands together, a sadness weighing on her as the magic did not thrum as it used too.

Melanie came sidling over, sliding her arm through Mammet's own. "My dear girl, something is bothering you. A year you've been here and that flower of yours, it grows and grows. But lately, it is beginning to wane. Do you miss someone? Harry and I did not upset you, did we? Everything is okay with that precious baby?"

Mammet gasped and covered her mouth. "Of course not, Melanie. No, I just am tired lately. But I love it here. This place, these children, it is all I have ever wanted, truly. And Ruby is fine. Happy as a lark."

Melanie reached over and held her arm. "Was it worth it, Mammet? To leave your world and come to ours?"

Mammet turned with a gasp and stared at her old friend. "W-what?"

Melanie smiled. "Oh Mammet. I have known since you came here. I have been alive for some time. I can read a fairy a mile away. My husband and I, we are the protectors of that door. The last guardians to lead the fae in this part of the realm. You think it was a coincidence he was there?"

Melanie sighed and squeezed her arm tighter, but with kind fingers. "I would have told you sooner, but yours was a burdened transition, and I did not wish to make it worse. We have guarded that door for centuries, my family and I. But the fae, they quit coming."

Melanie's lip trembled, but she took a deep breath. "Quit coming through the door. For years, centuries, I would go every day, different looks, of course, over the years, but eventually, I gave up. But my Harold, he never gave up. Always went there, hoping they would come again. Hoping to see one more pretty fae to lead here. To help transition."

Mammet sighed and then smiled. "I should have known. I had heard of guardians, but I thought they were long gone."

Melanie sighed. "Most of us are. We are the last, and I think there will be no one to take over. The fae have truly gone from us, haven't they? It was clear in the sadness you bear. You wait for someone, but you do not long to go back. So, I ask you again, Mammet. Was it worth it to lose your magic and your wings?"

Mammet smiled and nodded. "Yes, Melanie, it was worth it."

Mammet smiled again, but deep inside, her heart sunk. Her flower was beginning to wane as her magic did. All too soon, the spark of what made her a fae would end. She would

48

be nothing more than a mortal, and then her Nabiuma would not find her. She curled the shaking fingers into her apron. He had not come this long, maybe he never would. She quickly brushed at her cheeks and tugged on the sweet older lady's arm.

"Come now, Melanie. I want some of that peanut butter nut crunch ice cream. Ruby, she always likes to share with me."

Melanie laughed. "You mean you pretend to share and let her eat it all. But yes, let us move on to better things today."

The older woman slapped her arm with a playful grin and shifted, walking toward her prep table.

Mammet took the time to wave at the little girl that leaned against Harold's knee. Her fingers in her mouth, sucking on them. The pudginess of toddlerhood had not quite faded from her gaze, and the green of her eyes reminded Mammet of Nabiuma. And she longed for him; he loved children as much as she did.

She smiled at the girl and searched her tiny face. Smiling at the dimples that sunk into her cheeks and the sweet eyes that blinked up at her.

The child's interlocking fingers were removed from Harold's knee, and she ran toward Mammet, grasping her by the legs. "Mama. Harry telling me 'bout angels."

Mammet bent forward and brushed the girl's black curls from her face, framing her mocha face in her hands. "Oh really? What about angels?"

Ruby giggled, leaning into her mother's hands. "'Bout der wings and how dey watch over little children. I tol' him it was like the fairy stories you tell me."

Mammet folded her into a hug, pillowing her cheek on the girl's downy head and squeezing her little shoulders. "I love to tell you stories."

Ruby giggled and touched her mother's cheek. "Specially 'bout fairies."

Mammet smiled and nodded. "Yes, especially about fairies."

Mammet brushed her fingers along the girl's hair again, marveling at the softness between her fingers and the overwhelming love that dug deep within her heart and overflowed. She had come to the mortal realm to be near children. She had not expected her heart to be taken over by one so fully and her own little flat above the parlor to be either. It had been love at first sight when she saw the toddler a year ago as she was carried into the parlor, her large green eyes wide and staring at the world around her.

She had happily crowed that it was her birthday and she loved, "P'anut butta." Mammet stood, a slow smile making her face glow. When she had found out that sweet Ruby was up for adoption, she had not hesitated to take the little girl. The sweet thing that reminded her so much of her Nabiuma, while at the same time showing her how the mortal realm was magical as long as a child laughed.

Ruby stuck her fingers back in her mouth and lifted her eyes, looking around her mother's legs at the peanuts that sat against the door. She clapped her still stickily wet hands and laughed.

"Oh yay, Pa'nut butta crunch."

Mammet patted her daughter's head and shrugged her shoulders and bent to the task of picking up the nearby peanuts, carefully carrying them toward the table that Melanie stood at. She was startled from her task by Melanie's sharp intake of breath.

"My lands." She waved her hand in front of her face. "I believe, Mammet, that one more came through the door."

Mammet lifted her gaze, and she stared at the long limbs encased in blue jeans and the green eyes that searched the crowd looking for anyone to tell him where to go. Their eyes met, and Mammet stared long and hard, her breath catching in her throat. Time stood still as he moved forward, carefully watching his steps around all the children that filled the space.

He stopped in front of Mammet and cleared his throat. Mammet gave him a gentle smile and bent to reach between her knees, pulling Ruby from her leg. She held her up and, meeting his gaze again, spoke softly. "Nabi, meet Ruby. My daughter."

Nabiuma's eyes got wide and then he smiled, holding out his hand. His smile grew in size when the little girl grasped his fingers.

"Hello, Ruby."

Ruby giggled and tugged at his fingers. "Hi, Nabi."

Bêtes et Beautés

Jaap Boekestein

I guess you all heard the tale. About my beautiful sister, and the bargain papa made with the Beast. Yes, you know the story, I can tell.

You don't know the *whole* story, let me tell you that.

Beauty – that wasn't her real name, but Papa always called her that, and so did we – wasn't alone in the castle. No, she...

No, I am getting ahead of myself.

I need to start with the beginning.

It all began years ago, long before Papa got ruined and lost his way in the winter woods. Ten years ago, fifteen maybe, twenty? It all started with when the Beast became the Beast.

Good.

Once upon a time, there was a prince.

Now this was a handsome prince, living in a castle, with his court and his servants.

Yes, yes, yes, he will become the Beast! Patience! I will get to that.

Handsome, rich and powerful. A combination which seldom brings out the best in people, and it sure didn't with this prince. He was also rather young, so maybe that is an excuse. They say wisdom grows with the years.

For some it does, anyway.

He caught the eye of a fairy princess while he was riding in the woods.

She followed him as falcon; she followed him as fox.

She confronted the prince as herself: all beautiful, all magic, terrible and lovely, sweet and cruel. Fairies are like that. Long green hair that danced in the wind. A dress made of diamond raindrops, leaving her breasts uncovered, like the women of Crete used to have in the olden days. Her nipples were the dark green of oak leaves in late spring. On her throne of thorns and lilies she smiled, revealing needle teeth. "Good day to you, prince."

She didn't bow. She was royalty after all.

"Good day to you, fair lady," answered the prince, taking off his hat with an elegant gesture.

He knew how to impress the ladies.

"Come lay with me," the fairy princess invited him. She knew what she wanted; why waste words with this mere mortal?

The prince did not answer, but he approached her, his hands busy with his codpiece.

She opened her legs, her water dress split like the Red Sea split for Moses. A bed of green curly hair, but her lips were red rose petals, full and lush. Moist.

His codpiece was gone.

Oh my, he impressed the lady. He did.

He took her in his arms.

Kissed her lips.

His lance pierced her rose.

Yes, they fucked.

They fucked each other six ways to Heaven and seven ways to Hell. She screamed for joy, called him words in languages long dead, she let him ride her like... like...

You get the picture.

What vigor this mortal man had!

How limber, experienced and *slutty* this immortal lady was!

Afterwards, when he was sweaty and tired and had a big smile on his face, she reached between her legs. Her hand came back with a rose.

"Take it." No explanation.

The prince did.

She transformed herself in a whirlwind of leaves and left, utterly satisfied.

The prince returned to his castle.

The arrogant, young fool.

That night, he fucked one of his court ladies, from behind, and gave her the rose. She meant nothing to him.

The rose of the fairy princess.

Damned fool! Arrogant bastard!

The fairy princess found out, of course. Her anger lit up

the sky. Thunder and lightning!

She cursed the prince.

He became the Beast.

His castle a haunted place, his prison.

She threw the rose at the Beast's feet. "As long as you are a Beast, this flower will bloom and you will stay a Beast, until you truly love somebody and are loved back by the same person."

The fairy princess knew nobody would ever love him. Never ever. The Beast was ugly on the outside and on the inside. He would be cursed forever.

So that is how the prince became the Beast.

Many years later, when the prince was forgotten and the Beast had grown older and maybe wiser, my father spent one night in that cursed castle.

He ate, he drank, he slept, he enjoyed the hospitality of his unseen host.

Papa walked right into a trap. I am sure of it.

He took the rose as a gift for Beauty.

"You stole from me!" the Beast roared. "I will let you go if you send me your daughters."

"I will!" Papa cried.

You noticed the Beast said 'daughters'? Plural.

So that is how Beauty and I, her not very special sister, ended up at the gates of the castle.

By the way, my name is Anne, but that is not really important. I am not ugly, but rather common. Men see Beauty and forget I exist.

I learned to live with that.

I think that is what saved me ultimately.

Beauty and Anne held each other's hand for support. The mysterious coach that brought them to this old, dark castle had left. They were standing in the courtyard, in the somber darkness and chilling rain. Their cloaks were getting wet and heavy.

"We have to enter," Beauty said. "Otherwise, he will kill Papa."

"What... what will it do to us?" Anne asked. They had cried, both of them, on their way here. Now there weren't any tears left, just fear.

The great door opened, all by itself, magically.

One dancing light, a little flame hovering in the air, beckoned them.

The two girls entered the castle.

They didn't notice the hooded figure of the Beast, watching them from the deepest shadows. Was he waiting there to tear them apart?

Maybe?

But he saw Beauty, and his claws sheathed.

His tail flicked forth and fro.

O yes, without even knowing, or trying, she had caught him. Right there and then.

Nobody, neither girls nor the Beast, noticed the white owl looking down from the rafters. She studied all three of them, like they were pieces on a chessboard.

When all were gone, the girls to their dusty, cold rooms and the Beast to his lair, the fairy princess flew away. The

Beast had been cunning; he got himself some women.

O those traitorous mortals!

Imprison a girl.

Feed her lavishly for half a dozen days.

Dress her in the most beautiful dresses.

Leave little presents for her to find: jewelry, magical knickknacks.

Stay aloof.

Oh, she will get curious. Her mind will start to work, painting pictures, filling in the blank spots.

The girl will start to explore the castle, looking for her mysterious host. Especially when her common sister – the bore! – is too afraid to appreciate the food and dresses and presents.

The Beast watched Beauty, walking down the old corridors: a sweet dream, so beautiful.

The fairy princess watched both Beauty and the Beast, in the form of a mouse, a spider, a swallow, a cat and what not.

She watched and brooded.

A bath.

The castle had a bath: a pool of white marble, brass lion heads spewing hot and cold water, a beautiful collection of colored bottles, filled with oils, perfumes, essences, salts and herbs. Seven of the eight walls were mirrors, as was the ceiling. A fleet of floating candles provided enough light to see oneself a thousandfold.

Sitting on the edge of the bath, Anne was combing Beauty's long hair.

"When I am in the garden, I have the feeling I am being watched," Beauty said.

"By whom? By... By *it*?"

"By *him*," Beauty corrected her sister. "He is not an animal. He talked to Papa."

"Parrots utter words, but that doesn't make them a person."

"Has he hurt us? Doesn't he provide us with all these beautiful things?" Beauty said, a bit defensively. Why was Anne always so negative? "I don't think he means us harm."

"It has imprisoned us! We are alone in this dreadful castle."

"I don't feel we are alone. I know he is here." Beauty pulled herself loose and let herself float in the still warm bath.

Her perfect, perky breasts were little white islands in a dark sea.

In spite of the confident words of her sister, Anne shivered. "You scare me! I am going to bed." She rose and dried herself off. "Are you coming?"

"I will stay for a while," Beauty said dreamily. She looked at herself in the ceiling mirror. She could see her whole body. Her untouched body.

How would a lover's hand feel on her skin?

How would a lover's kiss feel on her lips?

How would a lover's love feel... *there*?

Beauty closed her eyes and floated, thinking about hands and lips and other things.

All the mirror walls were clouded by now, except one, as if there was an empty space behind the glass.

Of course there was.

Through the glass, the Beast was watching Beauty.

The little green spider watched both.

"I have seen him!" Beauty said during breakfast.

Anne almost choked on her bread. "Where? Here?" She looked around as if that terrible Beast would jump from behind the curtains, all claws and fangs.

"In my dreams."

"You are wicked!"

"Maybe I am." Beauty didn't specify her dreams.

Beauty climbed the stairs of the tower, round and round she went.

She was being followed, she was sure of it.

No, she didn't hear his steps, she didn't see his shadow, she didn't smell him, but she *knew*.

Would she dare? Would she?

Yes. She needed to know.

Beauty had reached the top of the tower. It was an old tower, crumbling, whole parts of it gone.

The wind played with her hair, her dress. She shivered, but she wasn't cold.

She stood with her back to the door opening. The woods

surrounding the castle stretched as far as the eye could see.

Beauty stepped forward.

She was standing on the edge now.

Old, brittle masonry. She knew. She knew exactly what she was doing.

Beauty screamed when the stone edge under her feet gave way. She swung with her arms; she was going to fall to her death.

The Beast was quick as lightning.

His powerful claw closed around her slender wrist. Saving her.

Beauty looked up and saw the face of the Beast.

She smiled.

They didn't notice the falcon circling the tower.

Learning to speak again, to look a beautiful girl in the eye, to treat her like a lady, to walk with her in moonlit gardens.

After fifteen years of solitude, and anger, and madness, and penance, the Beast had to relearn all those things.

Luckily, he was a quick leaner.

Or maybe Beauty was a great motivator.

Probably both.

Beauty looked at the Beast. He was so big. So hairy. So strong. His claws could easily rip her apart. His fangs could tear her throat in a quick heartbeat. He smelled of wild things.

And still...

He was respectful and polite.

He only touched her hand, so tiny compared to his.

His touch made her knees weak and her throat dry. She felt a strange fire in her belly. Was it magic?

Yes, the oldest one. The one without witches and wizards, or fairy queens or gods.

When he said goodbye, he didn't dare to embrace her. No, it wasn't modesty. This Beauty, she looked so frail, so delicate, he was so big, so strong.

Deny a man, any man, companionship for fifteen years and present him the most beautiful creature he has ever seen. He had lured her to his castle, but she had imprisoned him with the batting of an eye.

Beauty felt his hesitation. She stood on her toes, grabbed one of his fangs and pulled his head down. She kissed him.

Hidden in the shadows, Anne suppressed a cry of fear. What was her sister doing? Had she gone mad? How could she touch the Beast? How... How could she *kiss* that thing?

Anne stayed quiet as a mouse while both Beauty and the Beast went their own way.

They both looked back at each other, catching each other's eyes. They both hurried away. Confused? Afraid? Excited? *Hopeful?*

No doubt all of that.

Anne leaned against the wall, tears running down her face. What was to become of them? Beauty had gone mad! She was a fool; she didn't see the danger. They would never be saved, and in the end, the Beast would devour them all.

The black cat with the green eyes appeared from under the bushes it had been hiding in. In two, three slow breaths, the cat grew and transformed into a green haired, naked woman.

A startled cry escaped Anne's mouth.

The fairy queen turned around, her eyes a burning green fire.

Anne wanted to flee but couldn't.

The fairy queen looked at her. "Who are you?"

"I am Anne. I... I am Beauty's sister."

The fairy queen nodded slowly. "O, you are. Yes."

"Who... Who are you? Are you a devil?"

"A devil?" Now the fairy queen laughed. Surprisingly, she sounded a lot like a young woman, about Anne's age. "No, no. I am not one of your devils or demons. I am... No, my name would mean nothing to you, neither where I come from. I have been called a fairy by your people, and that will suffice." The fairy queen reached out and one of her long fingers caught the salt droplet on Anne's cheek. "Why do I see tears, Anne? Don't you like the Beast and his riches and magics?"

"My sister likes him," Anne answered cautiously. The touch of the fairy woman had been warm, like a cat's pawn.

Again, that fairy laughed. "But not you. Don't worry, Anne. I am the one that cursed him. He won't harm your sister. He needs her safe and sound."

"For what?"

The fairy queen shook her head. "Goodbye, Anne."

She became transparent and in a mere three moments, she was completely invisible.

Surprised, Anne squeaked like a mouse. It took her five minutes to compose herself and return to her room.

She passed by Beauty's chamber and opened the door to

say goodnight.

Beauty was asleep, a smile on her face.

Anne closed the door again and went to her own room.

It took a long time before she fell asleep.

Invisible to all, the fairy queen sat at her bed, watching the young girl.

The ignored sister. Such an old, old story.

Anne tossed under her sheets, her dreams filled with dread.

The fairy queen put her hand on the girl's head, calming her.

An invisible orchestra, playing old dancing tunes.

Swirling, in each other's arms.

Beauty and the Beast.

Looking each other in the eyes, feeling each other's bodies. Movement, heartbeats.

Dancing meant so many things. It could be a promise, a prelude, a seduction.

It all was.

The fairy queen should have been watching the Beast, brooding over his scheme to break the curse.

She wasn't.

She was watching the ignored sister, that Anne.

Anne was sitting in a window, listening to the music that haunted the grounds of the castle. She didn't dare to go and find out where it came from. No, she didn't *want* to know. From the window, she had seen Beauty hurry when the first notes sounded, as if she was called.

Anne knew what was calling Beauty.

"You want to leave?"

This time, Anne suppressed a cry. She turned her head and looked at the fairy queen.

"Not without my sister."

"But what if she wants to stay?"

"She is in love, she is blind. Blind to the dangers."

"There are no dangers. He won't hurt her. O, he was a stupid man, once. Because he was cold and cruel, I turned him into what he is now. But he won't harm your sister. I guarantee you that. He is in love, and she is his redemption."

Anne closed her eyes, said softly, "I cannot leave her. Don't temp me, please."

The fairy queen sat in the window with Anne. She touched the girl's hair. "I would like to temp you, Anne. In so many ways."

Puzzled, Anne looked up. What...?

The fairy queen kissed her.

Not on the cheek, not on the forehead.

No, on the mouth.

Lips on lips.

Tongue.

When did anyone love Anne?

O, people liked her, and sure, Papa loved her, of course!

She was his daughter. But for everyone else, she was always Beauty's sister. Everyone liked Anne, but everyone *loved* Beauty.

Beauty wasn't cruel. Never! She loved Anne and Anne loved her back, but in the end, Beauty was Beauty and Anne would always be Beauty's sister.

Did Anne dream to be loved?

Not really, those dreams died so long ago. She would always be the other sister, the common one. Maybe one day she would marry someone common, maybe she wouldn't and turn into an old spinster. Forever the sister.

Anne didn't expect love and certainly was not prepared for it.

Now... The love of the fairy queen was fickle and spontaneous, but also true and deep. Besides, she was beautiful and a damned good kisser.

Anne was swept away and returned the kiss.

The bed was huge, a heap of silk and fur and goose feather filled cushions.

She, Beauty, sat on him, the Beast. Fully dressed, still. White, like a wedding gown, adorned with pearls and lace.

They had kissed; they were hot.

"I want you," Beauty whispered. O damned, how much she wanted him! The fire in her belly burned, her heart raced, her blood boiled. "Take me!"

For all his power, for all his experience, for all his cumulated wisdom, the Beast didn't know what to do. He wanted her. O by all angels and devils, yes! But how could he fuck something so delicate, so fragile? If he let go, one moment was enough, he would certainly hurt her! You can't touch a flower with a sledgehammer. You can't light a candle in a hurricane.

She took his hand – no, claw – and put it on her bodice, just above her heart.

"Take me," she asked. Begged.

He looked her in the eye. Was it fear? Yes, fear of what he could do.

"Please, take me." She urged him on.

He wanted... He couldn't... Damn that fairy witch! She had cursed him with a body unable to love. He was the Beast, she a mere woman. He would be her death if he gave in!

"Take me!" Beauty cried out.

She slapped him, all her force and frustration focused in that little hand, right on his big nose.

Which was a pretty sensitive part of his anatomy.

He exploded with a red rage.

His claws emerged, ripping the bodice of the priceless dress apart. He roared, he grabbed her, took her.

He was the Beast.

She was Beauty.

She drowned and laughed in his force, she whipped up his violence by biting, scratching, beating him. By *challenging* him.

He was terrible and savage.

She was so delicate, so petite.

But so much stronger than he had thought. She welcomed his claws and fangs and body and... well, *that*. Scratches, bites, blood – Yes, Beauty *was* a virgin.

They fucked and fought as wildcats.

Beauty and the Beast.

But it was hard to tell which was which.

"I... I don't know," Anne whispered. Somehow, she was back in the big bath. Not with Beauty this time, but with this strange green haired woman.

The water's embrace was warm, and the fairy queen's embrace was hot as the summer wind.

"Shh, I do. Just enjoy."

The fairy queen's fingers circled over Anne's body, unlocking unknown – undreamed! – sensations. Her green lips nibbled Anne's earlobe, her long tongue just...

Anne groaned. *By all saints and angels!* What was she feeling? Why did this creature do this to her? She was not beautiful, she was not special. She didn't deserve this... *Ow, Mother Mary! What...?*

"You are so lovely," the fairy queen said in between kisses. She was slowly making her way down Anne's body. Every kiss was like a hot flame added to an already roaring fire deep inside Anne. "The fools were blind not to notice you. You are so sweet."

Suddenly, Anne cried.

Sadness?

Frustration?

Joy?

Relief?

A bit of all these.

Hot tears ran down her face. She hid her face in her hands. *O what a fool I am! I don't want to cry! She will get angry and...*

"Hush." Two arms embracing her, rocking her softly. "Hush, sweet Anne. Everything is fine. I am here."

Wildly, Anne shook her head. "I... We... Beauty is... I cannot..." she said from behind her fingers.

The fairy queen took Anne's wrists and with soft persuasion, she opened her hands to reveal a face covered with tears. "Let go, my love. Beauty can look after herself, don't worry about her. You have my word on it. She won't come to any harm. It is just us here. I want to love you and please you, because you are worth loving and pleasing. I am..." The fairy queen chuckled, "Fickle. O yes, I am. But my love is always true, and now I love you. Let me please love you, Anne. You are worth it."

"Yes?" Anne whispered. "Really?"

"Yes. Really. Let me show you."

The fairy queen started to kiss Anne's tears away.

Anne responded. Relieved, happy, excited.

In the bath in the room where seven of the eight walls were mirrors, the fairy queen and Anne, who had a sister, loved and fucked.

Nobody was watching.

The four of them met in the Great Hall of the castle.

Beauty on the arm of the Beast. She only wore a half open house coat. Her hair was undone, her lower lip was swollen, a bloody scratch on her cheek. Her cleavage showed bruised skin, purple and yellow.

She smiled. She was happy.

Anne stood next to the fairy queen. Fully dressed and somehow... more *composed* than ever before. She was Anne. Yes, she was Beauty's sister and always would be, but first she was Anne. Loved and thus lovely.

The fairy queen looked at all of them. She wore the diamond rainbow dress, the same she wore so long ago, the day she met a young, foolish prince in the woods.

"I see you have found love, true love," the fairy queen said. There was no malice in her voice. She was the fairy queen; she was fickle. "I will lift the curse." She raised her hand.

"Your majesty." Beauty stepped forward and bowed. "Please forgive me, but we have a request, the Beast and I."

The fairy queen raised an eyebrow. "Tell me."

You all heard the tale. How Beauty and the Beast lived happily ever after in the castle.

I assure you they do. They truly love each other.

I? I am Anne, I told you that.

The love of a fairy queen is fickle. She is aware of that. We had three lovely years together, but it didn't last. We parted as friends, and she gifted me three chests full of gold.

Nowadays, I live in a big house in a busy port city. I am patron of the arts and sciences, receiving poets and painters, writers, philosophers and scientists. I have lovers, men and women, and I am happy.

On moonlit nights, I sometimes think about my sister and her lover, and my own precious love. Ah, such sweet memories!

You noticed I said 'Beauty and the Beast', not 'Beauty and the prince'?

My, you are sharp!

My sister is still beautiful, I guess. With hair and fangs and claws.

She fell in love with the Beast. Not with some prince.

So that was her request. To become the Beast's equal.

My fairy love granted Beauty her wish. I guess she was in a pretty good mood.

Well...

Now you know it, the whole tale.

Care to share a bath with me?

I think you look beautiful.

The Brothers Doran

John A. McColley

Stuffy air filled Mab's great hall. Hundreds of fae milled about, wings buzzing, driving home the feeling of summer. Shifting shoes and hooves on the hard-packed dirt floor leant a background patter. Conversation rounded out the acoustic ambiance, filling the space with laughter, gossip and opinion on innumerable subjects. In moments, the queen would make her Solstice address. Wisps flitted near the ceiling, granting shifting, colored light. Mushrooms and root-knees provided seating.

Trumpet and drums announced Mab's approach. Everyone stood. The tone of conversation dropped to the occasional whisper. White light from Mab's glamored dress spilled into the hall, stilling the most persistent voices. Those with knees fell to them. All bowed.

"It seems to Us that We were gathered here only moments ago to celebrate with Our court, Our friends and family," Mab lilted. "It does Our heart good to see so many able to attend in good health."

"You are the sun which lights the world," intoned a chamberlain in response. Indeed, Mab spent her days outside of court weaving powerful spells which held the fae in the world. The minds of men had twisted and tilted in recent centuries, making life as a fae more tenuous and uncertain. Would they see another millennial ball? Another centennial? Only if Mab could hold the threads in the warp and weft of her magic.

"You are the fen and garden which gives Us cause to shine. In moments such as this-" The silence which had built around the traditional speech shattered as a guest fell over, toppling into the next without sign of trying to catch himself. The next also fell, stiff as a board. The trend continued, culminating in the thunderous crashing of horns and drums as their players fell, instruments clashing against each other, then the cavern floor.

The few guards unaffected by paralysis stepped into formation around the queen while she herself threw up a gleaming aura. Others still able to move gasped and clutched loved ones to themselves, dropping mugs and chalices of green wine. In one corner of the hall, a tittering broke out, growing to a chuckling as other voices joined in. Five figures rolled on the packed earth, guffawing and pawing at each other. An overzealous slap was rejoined with a fist to the wrong jaw and merriment turned to brawling.

Mab glided forward, her depleted entourage falling into step around her. She stood a few feet from the lunatic row, saying nothing for long minutes, for she was timeless and timelessness brings patience. Declan, eldest of the Brothers Doran, caught sight of the guards, then of the queen. He pushed his way to his feet, cuffing Fergus and Liam as they grabbed his legs.

"Get up, you fools!" he tried to say, but found himself without voice. He grabbed fistfuls of red and brown hair and hauled upward. Once the three stood, the remaining two realized something had happened and joined the others, patting themselves off and straightening clothing. They presented variations on a similar face, their father's face. Similar to other Amadán, they had long, thin noses, large, round ears and small, dark, beady eyes set into angular faces. They had mustaches or beards, both or none, in red and brown, mostly, though Eamon, the second youngest, was dirty blond.

"Amadán, my Stroke Lads," Mab said in a quiet, steely voice. "Since Seamus left you boys on your own, it's nothing but pranks and tussling. This display is a reflection of every day you pass, as We understand. Pranks We can appreciate. It is our way, as fae, though one might have allowed Us to finish Our convocation before stunning and toppling Our guests." At this, five disheveled heads bowed. The Amadán stared at the earth beneath their feet.

"Fighting, however, in this place, is not to be tolerated. This holy hall has been a symbol of camaraderie, unity and peace for as long as it has stood." As Mab spoke, her voice grew sharper, so cold, the breath of those around became like clouds. Most present expected a flash of light, of ice, something, striking the Lads dead where they stood. "Generals have met here, signed treaties, ended wars which spanned centuries here. Spells woven in golden sunlight and silver moonlight have held here for untold ages. The covenant of this place has held off the most fell monstrosities from the Deep Fae." The queen paused, collecting herself, beginning again, softly. "You are a family. You are bound by more than lineage, or should be. This is of utmost importance, especially here. Here, this is the first drop of blood spilled in all of Time." Mab pointed to a tiny spot of red on Eamon's shirtfront. A second drop escaped the end of the fae's pointed nose. Mab waved a hand, turning away. Before the drop struck the ground, every fae was whisked away, every lamp and platter removed. The Stroke Lads stood alone in the dim, damp, cool space below the earth, contemplating their sins.

"Now what do we do?" Cormac, the youngest of the brothers asked.

"Ye can do what ye like. Ah'm headed te McGinty's," said Declan.

"No dandelion wine, then?" Liam asked.

"Well, who's fault es that, then?" Eamon asked. "Ah didn't do this te m'self!"

"Push off ye little whiner!" Fergus said, combing his beard with his fingers and making for the exit on Declan's heels. Eamon sat on the packed dirt floor and pouted while the rest filed out with a relative minimum of shoving. He eventually felt drowsy and curled up his long stocking cap into a pillow.

Morning shot lances of bright light into the dark, empty hall. Dust motes danced lazily in the beams as Eamon stretched, stomach rumbling for lack of a feast the night before. Eyes still gummy, mind still hazed, he rose and started toward the exit. His foot met something yielding, yet heavy. As he kicked, it let out a grunt and rolled toward him. It pressed into his shins, forcing him to backpedal. He stumbled and fell over another slumbering form.

Wiping at his eyes, he saw one of the spots of light play over a familiar faded blue tunic. He leaned closer and scrutinized the slumbering fae's face. "Fergus!" The other's long beard was all atangle again, but he looked happy enough, until Eamon's calling of his name in surprise brought him around.

"Gah! What do ye want? Ah was havin' a grand dream wherein- Wait, how did ye find me en Sullivan's barn?" the older Amadán grumped.

"Ah di'n't. Ah never left the 'all, though Ah need to now. Pardon," Eamon said, trotting off to the exit with urgency.

"Stop all the noise!' Declan demanded, rolling over again. "Hey! Who stole mah bed?" he asked, sitting up and looking around.

"Lekly no one. Et's wherever ye left et. Look aroun'," Liam said, having himself fallen asleep in a field while watching the stars.

"The 'all?" Declan asked.

"The 'all?" Fergus and Cormac caught on, peering around. Eamon returned from his errand and the five fae stood in the midst of the dim great hall, confused and annoyed.

"But 'ow did we get back here?" Declan wondered aloud.

"Mab," Liam said. "Had te be."

"Well, Ah'm not enterested en such fooleshness. Ah'm goin' back to mah house en the bank o' the rever," Fergus said.

"Aye, et's home weth meh, too," Eamon agreed. They all nodded at this, separating and heading for their proper beds. The next morning, and the next, and the following that, they awoke together in the desolate great hall.

"She's stuck us all together en punishment for ruining her speech." Cormac caught on.

"Well, thes es a fine mess. Who's idea was the Domino Roll?" Fergus said, pushing his sleeves up to his elbows in preparation for a fight.

"Cool yer horses. You love the Domino Roll. We all do. Et's a classec," Cormac said.

"And et's beside the poin'. Doesn' matter whose idea et was. The prank wasn't the problem. Et was tha'." Liam nodded toward Fergus with his pushed-up sleeves. Fergus stared at Liam for a moment, then relented, nodded his head slowly and pushed his sleeves down.

"So what do we do?" he asked.

"Learn te get along?" Liam suggested. Cormac was the first to laugh, but the rest quickly joined, Liam included. He may have been the most insightful, but he wasn't above recognizing the humor of the situation. Fae might be mercurial, but they are also creatures of habit. True change didn't seem likely.

"Maybe we could do good deeds?" Eamon said once they'd begun to recover.

"Or make somethin' nice for Mab?" Declan offered.

"Or... nope, never mind, Ah don't hev an idea." Fergus jumped in, but sat back on one of the logs they'd rolled around their campfire just outside the great hall. They had thought all day, venturing off only to find food.

"We could make the most of et. We each want things from our homes, Ah'm sure. We can tek turns vesetin' each home and packin' up necessities to bring back here," Liam suggested.

"Ah don' want te settle en with you lot. Even ef we got along, we're five strong, grown Amadán. We should be lookin' fer wives, getting ready te hev little ones, not settin' up a frat house," Fergus said, crossing his arms.

"That may be, Fergus, but we hev te deal weth thengs the way they are. The facts are we're stuck together, we don' know 'ow te left the curse, and we're not lekly te do so anytem soon." They continued to discuss the situation through dinner and decided to go for a walk in the moonlight. Amadán love little better than a walk under the full moon. They could take their frustrations out on hooligans they found, or really anyone out late in the night, for who traveled so late who wasn't up to no good? Certainly some pranking would liven all their moods.

"There's one!" Fergus said, peering through the roadside bushes. While the moonlight was invigorating, and the fog in the hollows was an unexpected boon, the night had gone slowly. Few travelers were afoot.

"Shh! There's more than one. Ef you keep yer fool mouth shut, we can get 'em both!" Declan said, trying to exert his authority as eldest. Fergus released the clusters of leaves he'd been holding aside and turned on his brother, fists raised.

"Come on, Fergus, back off, don' mess thes up fer us. We can leave 'em wherever ye wan' after we've got 'em." Liam tried to bargain with his hot-headed elder brother.

"Mester Smartypants, always an answer fer everythen'! Ah'll show ye!" Fergus swung, but Liam was younger, faster, and had come to expect such responses from Fergus. He ducked into the bush. From the other side came a woman's cry. Fergus charged through the bush after his brother, and the rest followed.

In the rutted lane, bodies tussled, rolling over one another. Grunts and curses flew like flies around a summer stable. The Brothers laid hands on everything that moved, giving each other mild shocks and stunning anything else that got in the way. The tumult continued for some minutes before someone cried out, "Stooooooop!" Liam knelt over a form lying in the road.

"Ye got one! Ah got the other over there. 'Ad a purse on him fer some reason," Fergus said, swinging said article around his finger.

"Probably hers," Liam acknowledged.

"Ah! Ah lad an' a lass. We can hev fun posen' them!" Cormac said jovially.

"Not thes time," Liam said. "She's dead."

"Can we do that?" Eamon asked.

"Not generally, but et es our fault, ef enderactly."

"'Ow d'ye mean?" Fergus asked.

"She's been stabbed. Ef we'd have been payen' attention enstead of foolen' aroun', we meght ha' just got 'em and saved 'er. An' that's not all," Liam explained.

"Mab'll have our heads as et es! How much worse could et be?" Declan asked.

"She's... she was... pregnant. Ready to pop, Ah'd say," Liam said.

"No chance the baby could still be...?" Eamon asked.

"'Ard to tell, but ef et's gonna have a chance, we gotta get 'em out now," Liam said.

"Don' look at me," said Eamon.

"Gev me the knife," Fergus said. The rest breathed easier, let off the hook. The sound of rending flesh made the Brothers squirm, but Fergus was a hunter and knew his craft. In less than a minute, new cries pierced the air.

"Good lungs on 'em," Declan noted.

"Look 'ow 'e gleams," Eamon said. Indeed, the moon showed her full face upon the child's, the fluids still there making him shine bright.

"So, we've got 'em out. What do we do weth 'em? We're

78

no fet parents," Cormac said.

"Take the mother's shawl. Wrap 'em up," Liam said.

"After that, I men'," Cormac said. "We're leven' en an empty 'all under a great oak. We don' ha' furniture, let alone baby thengs."

"Find a doorstep?" Liam suggested.

"Don' see many choices. Once again, Liam 'as the answer," Declan said. They were agreed. They took what valuables they found on the robber and the woman and tied it all up in the robber's shirt. The rest of the brothers hung him in a tree, astride a large branch, and buried the mother beneath the tree, while Liam cooed to the baby, the valuables over his shoulder. An hour after midnight, he found a suitable house which seemed large and well-kept. The smells of good food wafted out the kitchen window.

Liam left the babe and its dowry on the stoop and knocked to alert those within to the child's presence. He then backed off across the road and watched from the bushes. A lamp lit in an upstairs window, and the curtain shifted as the occupant looked out. Liam hoped the other would investigate, seeing nothing from his angle. He watched impatiently for his plan to work when the ground began to tremble. It was noticeable only due to the extreme stillness of the night as first, but quickly became a repeated thump which rattled the windows of the house.

Turning, Liam saw a large troll trundling down the road with a goat across its shoulders. The shaking frightened the babe, and it began to howl. This drew the brute's attention. It stopped at the house, bending over to look at the source of the noise.

"A tiny thing, but perhaps a sweet enough dessert," the troll grumbled, shifting a bag which hung at its side forward. It scooped the babe and treasure up in one hand and deposited both in the sack, then turned, continuing on its way. Liam's eyes grew wide at the display. He couldn't let the night end in this fashion. He followed the creature for half an hour before coming to a deep ravine and the bridge which crossed it.

"Of course," he said to himself. "Should've realized where he was goin'. Ah've got to get the boys."

Liam turned and ran back down the road, then detoured to a small, abrupt hill topped with a flowering bush. As he stepped onto the hill, he spoke an ancient word and was back at the hall. The network of portals had been arranged before Mab's rule, but still served well. Two more hops and he was joining his brothers at the fated tree.

"'S about time!" Fergus said. "Did ye hold enterviews?"

"Ah left 'em lek Ah was sposed te, but-"

"But what? Et looks lek you've run the whole way back," Cormac observed.

"Aye, and we're going back now. A troll's found the babe before the master of the house could come to th' door!"

"Lovely," Fergus said, striking his shovel into the ground beside the grave. Without further comment, they followed Liam back through the portals to within sight of the bridge.

"Troll Bonegnasher!" Declan called out as they'd planned on the way.

"Ruu?" The gruff question came up from the depths beyond the moonlight's reach. "No Bonegnasher here. Begone before I eat you!"

"No Bonegnasher, you say? Et meh? Ha! Double ha! Ah had hoped te share thes bounty weth mah little brother, but ef he's not here, Ah'll move on. Et's too bad. These sheep are quite plump..." Declan pushed. The Brothers Doran hid in the brush.

"Wait! I like sheep! Don't go!" The ground shook as the troll vaulted up the stony walls, bouncing from one side to the other, finally leaping into the moonlight, jagged teeth and thin lips a mess with blood. "Where? Where are the sheep?" The troll demanded, seeing no one. He sniffed the air, searching for whoever had spoken. Declan waved on Liam and Eamon, who went to the brink and lowered themselves over.

"Ye've killed Bonegnasher ef ye lev under thes bredge, so how can Ah share a meal weth ye?" Declan said.

"The bridge and ravine below were empty when I found them, but I'm sure I would have bested this Bonegnasher," the troll bragged.

"Oh ho? Such a teny specimen as yerself? You thenk so?" Declan pressed, occupying the creature. "Why, Ah bet you couldn't pull up thet tree over there, the thick one!"

"No? I'll show ye how strong I am!" The troll howled, stomping over to the biggest tree it could see and wrapping its arms around the trunk. It groaned and heaved, cracking the roots. Another heave, and it was up, catching in the nearby boughs of other trees and shaking the forest, it seemed. "Rah! You see?"

"No, not that wee tweg! The beggest one, there!" Declan said, moving to a hiding place farther from the bridge. He led the troll on this way for some time. Many trees later, Cormac came up beside him.

"We've got the boy. Liam and Eamon are on the way back te the 'all weth 'em. They found a whole stack of wengs down there. Fairie wengs. Thes one's been eaten' what he ought'nt. Mab may be pleased to have 'em a statue, ef ye know what Ah mean."

"Done an' done, brother. Join meh?" Declan offered.

"Don' min' ef Ah do, brother," Cormac agreed. The two moved up behind the straining troll. Its great strength was running out after nearly a dozen huge trees. Mab wouldn't like losing those, but the wood could always be used, and the cause was just. Declan nodded at his brother and they both reached out, laying hands on the oaf's calves. Their power flowed out, seizing the troll's muscles. He froze, staring at the sky, arms wrapped 'round a tree, stiff as stone. Dawn would be there in an hour, well before the brute recovered. Then he'd be stone for good and eat no more faeries.

The brothers shook hands and jogged back toward the portal. In minutes, they were back at the hall, huddled with their brothers around the child, still wrapped in his mother's shawl and apparently none the worse for his trip into the troll's lair.

"What should we name 'em?" Eamon asked.

"Finn, Ah think," Liam said. "The way hes face shone en the moonlight spoke to meh."

"Finn Doran, a fitting name for a dweller in Mab's Hall," the queen said. The Brothers Doran looked up at the voice, eyes wide. The shock of a visit from she who had cursed them wore off after a moment. The five straightened, forming a line, leaving Eamon in the middle with Finn in his arms. "But this place is no longer mine... Let us call it Doran Hall."

All around, lanterns grew from roots crisscrossing the ceiling, ornate carpets rolled across the packed earth. Couches and tables and beds arose around the space now filled with color and light. "It seems you can work together, after all," Mab said. "The scourge of Callum Wood is ended. Faeries may safely roam again. The magic of the place will bloom as they tend it, lessening Our burden. You may live here, good Brothers Doran, as long as you will, and raise your son. We shall be quite interested in meeting him when he's grown. We have seen many faeries placed with mortals, but what will he become, with those tables turned?"

TRUE THOMAS

Cynthia June Long

In Scotland during the quiet years before the Wars of Independence, Thomas of Ercildoune, called the Rhymer, lived. A hawthorn tree shaded him as he lay upon a grassy hill near his home, composing songs while watching neighbors pull grayling from the Leader River. One day, a shining lady rode toward him on a milk-white horse.

The mare's mane, braided with silver bells, chimed as she drew near. The bridle gleamed gold. Astride her saddle, the Lady sat tall and proud. Her skirts were the finest silk, greener than grass. Her velvet cloak robed her in the sapphire sky and the jewels throughout her hair sparkled like the sunlight on the river.

Thomas bowed low. "You are as beautiful as an angel. You must be the Queen of Heaven," he stammered.

The Lady pealed a laugh like wedding bells. "I thank you for the compliment, but heaven is not the land I rule." Her voice was more melodious than Thomas's own harp. "Come with me now for seven years. Until you return, you must

84

serve me. Will you promise?"

Thomas tried not to be drawn into the deep eddies of her eyes. Her lips were as bold as the red lion of Scotland. "It would be my pleasure." He climbed behind her and circled her waist with his strong harpist hands. Leaning forward, he inhaled her sea-scented hair.

They galloped as fast as wind. Was it only one day or forty long nights? Thomas saw neither sun nor moon. They rode through deep rivers and passed underground. The sea roared.

His lady reined her horse at the top of a hill. "Look at the marvels I have to show you."

Three roads crossed. One was well-traveled and bordered by wildflowers. Briars choked a smaller path, narrow as a game trail, beset by brambles. The third wound down the middle of the hillside in a series of twists and curves. "Many ride the wide road of selfishness," she told Thomas. "It leads to the brimstone realm of Chaos and Darkest Night." She indicated the scant thorny trail. "Fewer choose generosity and service. The path to Righteousness may briefly snare." She nudged her palfrey toward the curved path in the center. Their horse cantered gently. "We are going to the Fair Lands, my home. I am Queen of Faerie."

Thomas inhaled his own voice.

"You have sworn," she reminded.

The Fairy Queen instructed Thomas in the rules of her land. "Eat only what I provide. The food of the Fair Folk is not meant for mortals, and those who eat of it can never return home. Await my word and speak to none."

Thomas nodded.

For seven years and a day, Thomas served the Fairy Queen in her unending twilight kingdom. Everyone he saw seemed young and beautiful. He played his harp at the

Queen's command and told stories none of the Fair Folk had ever heard. Thomas was treated like a prince at the Fairy Queen's side; when they danced, the entire court quieted.

Thomas smiled at all, but the prohibition against speaking prevented him from making friends. Tall courtiers mocked him with gifts of gold that crumbled to mulch overnight. Once the entire court departed for a hunt, leaving him alone in the emptied hall, forgotten like a dropped riding glove. His time with the Queen – her harmonic laugh, her encompassing smile, her radiant face shining like a lantern in their cavernous chamber – was his entire world. When she offered gifts of fresh bread, summer berries, and hazelnuts, Thomas embraced her like ivy clinging to an oak tree.

Seven years passed as quickly as a lily blooms and withers.

When the door to his chamber burst open like a thunderclap, Thomas knew his sojourn was over. The Queen rushed in and handed him a green velvet cloak. "You must leave now," she urged. "They will cast a servant into hell. I will not sacrifice you." They hurried to the stables through dark, winding passages.

"I'll never forget you," Thomas swore.

"No, you won't." They parted where they had met, beneath the hawthorn tree near Ercildoune. "Truly you have earned your wages," the Fairy Queen said. She grasped his cheek and delivered to his lips a lingering kiss that tingled like lightning. "I give you the gift of True Speech."

In Ercildoune, Thomas greeted his friends and neighbors. Hearty handshakes and indulgent smiles welcomed his return, but no one believed his story.

"Were you fighting in the war?" some asked. Scotland was contesting Norway's claim to the Hebrides.

"It's the truth!" Thomas insisted.

"Tell us another tale."

In the days which followed, Thomas once again leaned upon his harp. His minstrelsy flourished because all stories carry the heart of truth. He could recount the Norman Conquest and kings' histories of Malcolm, Alexander, and Macbeth so that his countrymen thought they were there. These tales he followed with romantic sagas that even brought furtive tears to gruff blacksmith eyes. A crowd favorite was his ballad of plucky Janet who rescued her cursed love from nearby Carterhaugh Woods.

"Where'd you learn that tune?" the steward of Dunbar asked.

Thomas found his tongue frozen to the roof of his mouth. "In another country," he managed.

One autumn, as the villagers turned out for the barley harvest, Thomas stationed himself beneath a wych elm to harp. "It'll rain hard tonight," he cautioned between songs, never looking up.

The sky was clear and cloudless, without any wind. The farmers, men who earned their livelihood gauging the skies, laughed. The next day, the heavy rains overflowed the Leader and Tweed riverbanks, flooding the fields and submerging the roads.

Thomas's renown grew. The laird of Bemersyde, Haig family patriarch, climbed the black hill to visit Thomas in his tower-house. "Will you teach my daughters to play the harp?" the laird asked.

"*Come what may, whatever betide, a Haig will be laird of Bemersyde,*" Thomas murmured. He beckoned to the wife and ten girls waiting in the overstuffed carriage on the heathered plain below. "The next one's a boy," he promised the mother.

"The midwife said there won't be any more."

But within the year, the family circled Thomas with a

yellow rock rose garland as they christened a son to inherit their estate.

In later years, Thomas often visited the Earl of Dunbar's table. Fragments of a dirge came to him unbidden one night, and he stopped his conversation abruptly to stare out darkened windows north toward Edinburgh. "*A mighty noon tempest shall shake Scotland's core,*" he intoned. The next morning was calm, and the Earl questioned Thomas; Thomas counseled patience. As the Earl sat down to the midday meal, a royal herald pounded his heavy castle doors.

The trumpet blast was heard in the center of town and even to the top of Thomas's Black Hill Tower. The death of Alexander III sounded across the Borderlands, blowing gales of grief across the country. A storm of successors followed, and an outbreak of hostilities with England.

By the Fairy Queen's gift, True Thomas could predict future days. As Scotland prepared for war, Thomas spoke of a union of crowns, rose and thistle entwined. England's King Edward massacred at Berwick and carried off the Stone of Scone, the seat of Scottish kingship; Thomas promised Scots and English would unite. William Wallace defended Stirling Bridge, and one year later, the calvary abandoned him at Falkirk, leaving Wallace to hide like a hare in the thickets; Thomas foretold a Scottish king. He assured the return of the coronation Stone.

Thomas lived long and well, trusting in the Scottish sovereignty he would not see. One new moon night toward the end of his life, a deer paraded through town prancing like a circus horse. Thomas left his room, locked his home, and followed the doe into the woods. The Fairy Queen was calling him.

His neighbors never saw Thomas again, but many believed he would return. They quoted his prophesies to build morale during the Second War of Independence, and Thomas was remembered throughout the next century and beyond. In three hundred years, Scotland would rejoice as James VI was coronated James I, King of Great Britain. Finally, in 1996, the Stone of Destiny would be delivered to Edinburgh Castle. Tourists today visit the ruins of Rhymer's Tower in Earlston, Berwickshire to await his expected return, when True Thomas will again bring trustworthy promises and warnings to new generations.

The Cafe at the End of the Lane

Vonnie Winslow Crist

Jack tried not to stare when the short, hairy man wearing an over-sized hat slid into a chair at his table. Instead, he finished off his beer and motioned for another bottle.

"Good evening," said the man.

Jack was relieved the man didn't extend a hairy hand expecting him to shake it. He supposed the guy was some sort of dwarf. Maybe homeless judging by the crudeness of his clothing. Probably the excess hair thing was related to his dwarfism.

"Looks like you're drowning your sorrows."

Priding himself on always being polite, never staring at those different from himself, Jack looked the hairy dude in the eye. "Lost my job today due to down-sizing, and now, I'm not sure how I'm going to pay my rent, much less the cost of college courses."

"Sorry to hear that." The fellow raised a finger, motioned for someone to come over and sit down.

A woman, about his age, slipped into the vacant chair directly opposite Jack. Though average in looks, he found himself staring at her. There was something magnetic about her eyes, almost as if they'd seen things no one else had seen and she was all the wiser for the experience.

"Cora," she said with a shy smile. "I see you've met my friend, Mr. Brown."

Jack nodded. He suddenly smelled pine and wild flowers, and felt the desire to smooth Cora's disheveled hair.

"I want to tell you about the day I first met Cora," said Mr. Brown. "Then, ask you a question."

He shrugged. "I have no one waiting for me at home and nothing better to do tonight. Tell away, Mr. Brown."

The dwarf smiled, bought him another beer, leaned close, and began to relate the tale. "Before going outside to pick up the branches that had snapped off her maple tree, Cora checked the weather report to confirm there were no more thunderstorms heading her way. Thankfully, the radar was clear. So she slipped on a pair of old sandals, slogged across the lawn, and bent down to gather some of the storm debris. It was then she spotted the bird's nest.

"The nest had been hurled to the ground and ripped into two wads of tangled twigs, grasses, embroidery floss, and hair. Cora suspected it was her hair and the left-over threads from her sewing that had been woven into the nest. She always tossed hair and floss into the garden for the birds to use.

"Cora gasped when she saw a trio of baby birds were scattered to the right of the nest. Ants had swarmed to the potential meals and now covered two of the nestlings. Both of them were obviously dead—but the third bird was alive and struggling.

"'No!' whispered Cora as she scooped up the newly-hatched bird and plucked red ants off of its naked skin. The ants, angry at the loss of fresh food, bit her fingers. Nevertheless, she persisted and soon found herself cradling a nestling who needed food, warmth, and constant care.

"She carried the bird inside, spread a scrap of flannel in a shoebox, placed the creature on the soft fabric, and gently swaddled it. The hatchling's eyes were closed, but its tiny beak opened every now and again. It needed food.

"Cora searched through her kitchen drawers till she located an eye dropper, a cutting board, a paring knife, and a plastic container. Next, she hurried to her bathroom medicine cabinet and grabbed a pair of tweezers. Finally, she snatched her gardening trowel from a hook by the backdoor and went outside.

"The soil in her herb garden was still wet from the rain, so it was easy to dig a shovelful of worm-laden dirt. Cora dumped a little of the earth and several wriggling worms into the storage container. Then, she went back inside to tend to the hungry birdling.

"Mincing worms turned out to be more difficult than Cora imagined it would be, but she continued chopping, and soon had a gelatinous mash ready to feed the baby bird. By trial and error, she found it took a combination of eyedropper and tweezers to get the worm mash and a little water down the nestling's throat. And as the helpless bird-child responded to her warm hands and careful feedings, Cora felt a spark of mother-love ignite deep inside her.

"'You need a name,' she told the birdling. Without the benefit of feathers, Cora had no idea what sort of bird she'd saved. And so many names depended on feather pattern or color. As she ever-so-softly stroked the hatchling, she thought how blessed the nameless creature was to still be alive.

"'Blessed!' Cora smiled. 'Blessed is the perfect name for me to call you.'

"After the first few days, Cora replaced Blessed's shoebox home with a box she'd picked up from the grocery store. Using a box-cutter, she cut large windows in three of the box's sides. Next, she scissored three rectangles of sheer netting and duct-taped them over the openings. Then, she taped one of the box's top flaps down. The other flap allowed for easy access, and both Cora and Blessed seemed satisfied with the more spacious bird-child residence.

"As the hours turned to days and the days added to weeks, Blessed thrived. His eyes opened, he grew pinfeathers, and his cheeping grew louder and more varied. Cora learned to detect the differences in tone and urgency in his voice. Sometimes, Blessed called for food, sometimes for warmth, sometimes for company. And Cora looked forward to taking breaks from her work to tend to Blessed's needs.

"Once Blessed was able to hop onto her finger, Cora took him outside early each morning to play beside her in the garden while she tended her plants. He never went far from her side. And if Blessed strayed more than an arm's length away, all Cora had to do was whistle. The bird-child would squeak and hurry back to her hand.

"When Blessed's true feathers came in, Cora saw he was a robin and realized it was time he learned to survive on his own. Robins didn't winter over in her part of the country. If Blessed was to live the life of a wild bird, he had to find his own food, strengthen his wings, and join those of his own kind on their flight south.

"Cora tried every technique she could think of to teach Blessed to find his own insects and berries. He would cock his head, watch her with a puzzled look, then cry for her to feed him. After a weekend of failed attempts, Cora sat crossed-legged with Blessed in her lap on a rock flanked by a rosemary plant and a pot of lemon thyme and cried. Her head was bent, and her eyes still blurry from tears when she felt someone tap her shoulder.

"'I will take him now,' said a deep, raspy voice.

When Cora saw who'd spoken, she couldn't suppress a small scream. The wrinkly-faced man who'd addressed her didn't seem surprised at her reaction. He waited ten or twelve seconds for her to scrutinize him before speaking again. And scrutinize him she did.

"He stood about two and a half feet tall and was clothed in short britches stitched from a rough fabric similar to burlap. Moss, leaves, and twisted roots adorned his pants and were twined into his straggly, copper-colored hair. His muscular arms ended in over-sized hands with stubby fingers. His bulbous nose overhung a wide, thin-lipped mouth. And though Cora was startled at the size of his pointed ears, it was the man's faintly glowing eyes that caught her gaze and refused to let it go."

"You?" asked Jack. The whole pointy ears thing would explain the over-sized hat. Of course, he was too polite to ask to see Mr. Brown's ears.

"Me," said Mr. Brown. "Now, back to the story."

"'Who are you?' Cora managed to ask.

"'Acorn Cap Brown Man,' said the hairy, little man as he reached for Blessed. 'And you can do no more for the robin. He must learn the ways of the wild from the creatures of the woods.'

"Cora nodded at Brown Man. She knew he was right, but she wasn't sure she could bear the quiet emptiness of her apartment without Blessed.

"'He's been such company for me,' explained Cora. 'I work from home.' She gestured toward the ground-level door behind her. 'I'm not supposed to have pets, so I feed the birds and squirrels. And of course there are my plants, but...'

"'He must learn the ways of the wild from the creatures of the woods,' repeated Acorn Cap as he extended one of his hands toward her.

"'Wait,' Cora begged. She held Blessed at eye level, then brushed his feathery back with her lips. 'I know it's for the best, but…'

"Blessed looked at her with his shiny black eyes, tweeted, then flew from her hand to the leathery palm of Acorn Cap Brown Man.

"'Child,' began Acorn Cap. 'You've saved and nurtured a hatchling. And your kindness deserves reward, but I have no treasure.'

"'I didn't adopt Blessed for reward.' Cora pulled a tissue from her pocket and blew her nose.

"The Brown Man nodded. 'Which is why you deserve one!' He spit on his thumb, and then swift as a lizard's tongue, swiped Cora's eyes with the spittle.

"'What are you doing?' Cora rubbed her eyes with the tissue. 'I can't believe you just—'

"The words she meant to utter next vanished from Cora's mind. She suddenly was able to see who lived in her garden. Amongst the butterflies flitting from lavender blossoms to sage blooms were tiny fairies with shimmering wings and twitching antennae. Several piskies sat on the edge of her birdbath, sailing leaf boats across the surface of its water. And not only did a toad squat beside a wide, shallow bowl of water she'd placed under the rosebush for the chipmunks, but a chubby gnome with a red stocking cap sat beside the amphibian.

"'You'll be lonely no more,' said Acorn Cap as he placed Blessed on his shoulder. 'Though perhaps, you'll come to regret my gifts.'

"With the swiftness of the wind, he stepped forward,

reached up on either side of Cora's head, and clapped his palms over her ears. When Acorn Cap removed his rough hands, Cora was able to hear the singing and chatter of the Fair Folk that surrounded her. And she heard fiddling, drumming, and flute trills coming from the gnarled oak behind her garden.

"'Now, go, child. Dance for a few minutes with them,' urged the Brown Man. 'The robin will return to you for a visit before he wings south.'

"Cora stood. She felt light-headed, like she'd sipped some champagne. "Thank you for helping Blessed and for…"

"The whirl of movement all around her lured her eyes away from the smiling Brown Man and cheeping Blessed. The piskies, gnome, fairies, and several Fair Folk who'd Cora hadn't spotted before beckoned to her as they skipped, twirled, or fluttered toward the oak tree. Her feet began to nimbly move in time to the rhythm of the drum. She laughed and polka-stepped toward the oak with a last glance over her shoulder at Acorn Cap and Blessed.

"'Remember to step from the ring before you get dansey-headed, child,' warned Acorn Cap Brown Man. 'And when you think of your own backdoor, you'll be able to return to it.'

"'I'll remember,' breathed Cora as she stepped into the center of a circle of red-capped mushrooms amongst a throng of joyous Fair Folk.

"As she began to spin and whirl to the staccato pulse of the tune, a swarm of winged creatures zipped around her head and the fat toad from beneath her rose bush frolicked at her feet. It occurred to her as the fast-footed reel grew wilder, that she'd already forgotten what Acorn Cap had told her to think of to return home.

"She tilted her head side-to-side, giddy with music, and

danced even faster. For a split-second, Cora fought through the euphoria and realized, now that she pondered it, she wasn't sure where home was. But the intoxicating notes of the pipes and fiddles filled Cora's ears till her head throbbed with music, and she closed her eyes. When she opened them, she noticed a hairy Brown Man grinning at her from beside a towering tulip poplar. On his shoulder perched a robin.

"The bird chirped, fluttered its wings, and stared at her with dark eyes. There was something familiar about the robin, something she couldn't quite recollect.

"'Cora, come dance. Cora, come dance,' chanted the throng of Fair Folk as they led her hop-skipping toward a sparkling stream at the edge of the forest.

"With footfalls lighter than dandelion puffs, she discovered only the soles of her feet touched the chilly stream water that rushed and tumbled over fallen tree branches and smooth rocks on its way to the sea. And as she glided into its vine-tangled, thickly-leafed, too-green depths with the Fair Folk, Cora heard the distant laughter of a Brown Man."

"It's a good story," Jack said as he glanced from Mr. Brown to Cora, "But seeing the fairies is a little far fetched for..."

Before he could finish, Mr. Brown took spit-wet thumbs and swabbed Jack's eyes. "What the..." And that's when he saw the gnomish men and women scampering across the cafe's floor. They caught the spilled drinks with tiny mugs and gathered the sandwich crumbs in miniature baskets. Hanging off the lamps were winged creatures of indeterminate sex. They seemed to be eavesdropping on the muttered conversations of the cafe's patrons. As he looked at Cora, he saw sprites, no bigger than butterflies, circling her head.

"Now, to hear them," said Mr. Brown as he clapped his hands over Jack's ears.

And hear the magical folk he did. There was laughter,

shouting, singing, and music.

"Why me?" Jack managed to say as his feet tapped under the table to the irresistible beat of the Faerie music.

"Because I was wrong," responded Mr. Brown. "Cora isn't happy without one of her kind to keep her company. And you seem a likely choice."

Cora had stood. Her feet dancing, she held out her hand to him and begged, "Please?"

"So will you go?" asked Mr. Brown as he walked to the back of the cafe and swung open an always-locked door.

Silver moonbeams illuminated a path from The Cafe at the End of the Lane's back door into the woods. On the path, a parade of gnomes, pixies, elves, and other magical creatures danced, sang, and played strangely-crafted musical instruments by the full moon's light. With only a moment's pause, Jack chose magic. He stood, grasped Cora's hand and waist, and waltzed her out the door.

Mr. Brown closed the portal, sat down, and finished Jack's beer. Deaf to the music, blind to the fairies, drowning in their drinks, and deep in their thoughts, no one in the cafe even noticed the couple's departure. Nor did they notice the robin who'd flown in the door and now perched on Acorn Cap Brown Man's shoulder whispering dark secrets into his pointed ears.

The Wish

Deborah Brown

Be careful what you wish for…

I should know. I'm a wish fairy. Fully trained, triple certificated. Ready, willing and able to grant a wish. Any wish. However, granting a wish isn't as simple as some people think. A wish fairy can't just go granting wishes willy nilly. We have to wait for that one special wish that is specifically attuned to us, and I had been waiting a long time, watching whilst fairies that had graduated behind me got to grant wishes of their own. Every day I would report to the wish bower, hoping that today would be the day I finally heard my wish, but time after time, I was disappointed.

This particular day I was sitting in the wish bower, more from force of habit than anything else. The wish bower is always full of the buzz of wishes, but unless a wish is meant for you, you can't actually hear it. All you hear is a low-pitched hum, like the droning of bees. It was nearly the end of my shift, and I was half asleep when I heard it. My wish. Loud and clear.

I wish I was dead.

The wish pulled at me, tugging me away from the bower, away from Faerie. I closed my eyes as I was drawn through the Vail, the barrier that separated Faerie from the shadows. I'd heard that it hurt, that passage to the shadows, but it wasn't so bad. At any rate, I was so excited to finally have my own wish that I didn't feel any pain.

I opened my eyes to find myself in a poky, ill lit room. There was a bed on one side, but my wish wasn't in it. My wish sat at a table with his head cradled in his arms.

"I wish I was dead," said my wish and lifted his head. He saw me, and his eyes widened.

"Jeezus," my wish said. "I must be drunker than I thought." He raised his hands and rubbed his eyes, then peered at me blearily. I gave him a smile.

"Frig off figment," he muttered and reached for the flagon that stood beside him on the table.

"Wassa matter, Ary?" came a woman's voice from the bed.

"Nothing," said my wish, taking a swig from his flagon. He glared at me.

"Go on. Shoo."

"I'm afraid I can't," I said apologetically. "You've made a wish, you see, and I am contractually bound to fulfil it." I reached into my coat and withdrew a document which I proffered to him.

"What's this crap?" He snatched it from my hands and studied it with bloodshot eyes.

"It's all quite legal," I offered helpfully.

He frowned at me. "This. Is. Crap. I never made any wish."

"Yes, you did. See, it's written right there." I reached over and pointed out the relevant line.

"I wish I was dead?" he ground out. "For Chrissake. *Obviously,* I don't wish I was dead. *Obviously,* I was speaking…metaphorically."
"Ary?" came a voice from the bed. "Who are you talking to?"

He ignored her. "Listen, this is stupid. For one thing, I'm drunk. You can't take anything a drunk says seriously. For another thing…I'm drunk. You are obviously a hallucination brought on by an acute attack of alcohol poisoning. Although…" His voice turned thoughtful. "You're a very pretty hallucination."

I shook my head. My wish leant across the table and touched my face. Only, of course, he couldn't. No one in shadow can truly touch anybody from Faerie. They can see us and hear us and whilst we can manipulate objects and events in shadow, we can't touch them either. I felt his fingers as a soft breeze against my cheek. He gave a grunt of satisfaction.

"See, you're not real." He turned to the bed. "Myra," he said. "Can you see anybody sitting here at the table with me?"

The woman in the bed sat up and peered groggily across the room.

"Only you, you great drunken sot. Are you coming back to bed?"

My wish turned back to me and raised an eyebrow.

"Not real," he said smugly.

I sat back and studied my wish carefully. He was kind of appealing in a big, muscular, drunken piggish sort of way. His long, black hair would have been nice if the ends hadn't been dipped in spilt wine. His dark blue eyes could have been magnificent if they were less bloodshot. His mouth would have been beautiful if it wasn't curled up into a sneer.

I shrugged. "Like it or not, I'm here to fulfil your wish, and I won't be going anywhere until I've completed my contract. I'll still be here when you've sobered up."

He sneered again. "Perhaps I'll just drink myself to death and save you the trouble." He reached for his flagon and raised it to his lips. He took a long swallow then spat it out with a curse, dropping the flagon to glare at me.

"Did you do that?"

"What?" I asked innocently.

"Change my wine into water."

"You look dehydrated. Water's good for you. Besides, that's *not* the way you're going to die – drinking yourself to death. This is my first wish, and it's going to be a good one. I've got something much more special in mind for you."

My wish gave me an incredulous look, and then shook his head. "I am not dehydrated," he said. "I'm demented. I'm holding a conversation with a figment of my imagination."

"My name is Qqrhqzytozqph," I said.

He stared at me blankly. "Jeezus," he said, lowering his head to his arms. Then he said in a muffled voice. "*If* you're still here when I wake up…I'll call you Fig. Short for figment." He lifted his head and gave me a crooked smile.

I smiled back. "Oh, I'll still be here." I said. "I've got big plans for you. What should I call you? Ary?"

He dropped his head back down again. "You can call me Sir Aryss."

The woman in the bed gave a shriek of laughter.

"Hey, Sir Aryss. If you've finished chatting with yourself, you can come and show me your lance. Come on, Ary, sweetie," she said coaxingly. "Come back to bed. I'm getting cold."

"Sod off," said Sir Aryss.

I sat and watched my wish as he fell asleep with his head cradled on his arms, my plans for his spectacular demise running through my head. First, that woman would have to go. My wish would have someone much grander to mourn his passing. Yes, I would get my wish a princess, and then I was going to turn Ary the drunk into Sir Aryss, the hero. If I had my way, they would be talking about his death for centuries to come. I sat back in my chair and waited for Ary to wake up. Then I could begin to put my plan into action.

One month later, I couldn't believe how well my wish was coming along. No alcohol and a rigorous exercise regime had honed Ary's already muscular body to heroic proportions. I'd ditched the witch in the bed and now Sir Aryss, clean and clear eyed, his long black hair tied back in a neat, shining queue, was ready for the next stage of his wish fulfilment.

There had been one brief period when Ary, unconvinced of the legitimacy of my contract, had balked.

"This is sodding ridiculous," he had snapped at me. "I *don't* want to die. Why do I have to do any of this? Give up wine. Give up *sex*, for Chrissakes. I don't have to do any of this!"

"Don't you?" I asked.

He stood there a moment frowning, a look of intense concentration on his face, then shook his head in baffled amazement.

"Sod it," he whispered hoarsely. "I *do* have to do it. Is it magic?"

"It's a wish," I answered. "A wish, once granted, must be fulfilled. There is no power in Faerie or shadow to gainsay it."

"Sod it," he said again, but after that, he seemed resigned to his wish, perhaps more so than I was. You see, we'd been warned about it, becoming attached to our wishes and to my consternation, against all my training and all my stern admonitions to myself, I found myself growing fond of Ary. Too fond. Oh he was stubborn and wilful, always questioning me about the direction my wish was taking, but he could be sweet and funny; he made me laugh. He had a wicked, slanting smile that would sometimes catch me unawares, making my stomach flutter strangely. He was definitely good to look at, and I spent a lot of time doing that. However, I would tell myself that all these qualities only enhanced his value as a hero and would ultimately lead to his death being so much more meaningful. Thus, armoured against any regrettable lapses in control, I put the next stage of my wish into action. It was time for Ary to catch his princess.

"Why?" he asked me.

I rolled my eyes. "It won't be just any princess, Ary," I said. "This one's going to be cursed."

"Oh joy," said Ary sarcastically.

"Then, when you lift the curse, you'll be a hero."

"And dead."

"Well, yes. Still," I said enthusiastically. "There will probably be time for a bit of…well, er…recreation before you die."

"Something for me to look forward to then," said Ary, but he didn't smile.

We were standing by the shores of a small, mirrored lake. I had brought Ary here to fulfil two tasks. One was to meet a princess. I had arranged for one to come riding down the shore of this lake very shortly. The second was to retrieve a weapon. A weapon of legend, fit for a hero to bear.

Ary gazed out at the lake. He wasn't entirely convinced about this phase of my wish.

"So, I take off all my clothes, swim out to the middle of the lake, dive down, find the sword, and then swim back? Sod it, Fig, it's the middle of winter. I'll die of pneumonia."

"That is *not* the way you'll die," I said firmly. "Titania's tits, Ary, don't be such a sook. When you have the sword in your hand, raise it up over your head and come up slowly. When you can touch bottom, walk onto shore. The princess will be here. When she sees you come out of the lake with Excalibur in your hand, she'll know that you're the one she's been waiting for."

"As long as she's only looking at my *sword,*" said Ary. "Since the other parts of me won't look too impressive after a dip in that."

He began to take off his clothes.

I blurted out without thinking. "She's stupid if she doesn't find every part of you impressive, Ary."

He paused in the middle of pulling his shirt over his head and gave me his wicked smile. Then his face stilled.

"I wish I could touch your hair, Fig," he said softly. "It's beautiful. Like sunlight and moonlight all woven together." He reached out and ran his hand down my hair. It felt like the lightest of summer breezes.

"I should think you've had enough of making wishes," I said, more sharply than I had intended.

His mouth tightened. "Yeah," he said, turning away to finish disrobing.

The atmosphere suddenly became decidedly chilly, and it wasn't just due to the frigid winter temperature. Ary stripped off and stood at the water's edge, shivering.

"Fig…" he began.

I held up my hand. "She's coming. Quick Ary, off you go."

He hesitated.

"Go!" Sometimes you've got to be cruel to be kind.

Ary threw me a dark look, and then plunged into the lake.

"Oh Jeezus!" he gasped.

I didn't have time to mollycoddle him although I did feel rather sorry for him as he stood shivering in the icy water. I crossed my arms and gave him a stern look.

"Ary."

I could hear the sound of fast approaching hoof beats. Ary stood for a moment looking at me. I couldn't read his expression, and it made me uneasy. Then he gave a shrug and, taking a deep breath, dived under the surface.

With a clatter of hooves and the jink and jingle of leather and metal, the princess and her retinue arrived at the lake.

She was pretty and plump with a wealth of red gold hair cascading from beneath her stylish cocked riding hat. She reined her palfrey to a halt and spoke to an older, grey bearded man riding beside her.

"I trust this won't turn out to be another wild goose chase, Marcus," she said. "I fear neither I nor my poor subjects can endure much more. If we don't find a true hero before noon tomorrow, then all is lost."

Noon tomorrow? I frowned. I hadn't planned for Ary to die so soon. All of a sudden, I felt very strange. There was a sick, fluttery feeling in my chest. I swallowed hard. *This is all quite normal,* I told myself firmly. *Your work here is almost done. It's natural to feel a little...* How did I feel? I should have been feeling pleased and proud at almost completing my first wish and in such a spectacular manner. Instead I felt anger and some other emotion I couldn't recognise.

"Get a grip, Qqrhqzytozqph!" I admonished myself.

The princess spoke again. "There is no one here, Marcus."

"But, Highness," said the grey bearded man. "I cast all the auguries correctly. Right here and right now is where your hero is supposed to be."

He looked around, and then spotted Ary's discarded clothing. Excitedly, he grabbed the princess's arm.

"There, Your Highness! See! Someone is here."

"Yes, but where, Marcus?" she said dryly. "Unless he's under the water..."

At that moment, Ary rose from beneath the lake, Excalibur held high in one hand. I had seen many wonders in Faerie but truly there was nothing to rival the glory of a wet and naked Ary as he emerged from the lake, his black hair hanging in sodden elflocks around his face. The princess certainly couldn't take her eyes off his…sword. Ary looked a bit blue around the lips as he knelt before her horse, Excalibur planted in the loose stones at his feet.

"Highness," he said. "I offer you my sword and my service. Do with them what you will."

I'd never noticed before what a beautiful voice he had. Low and raspy, like caramelised syrup.

"I thank you, Sir…?"

"Sir Aryss," Ary replied and smiled at her with that wicked slanting smile of his. It was then I recognised what that other emotion I had been feeling was.

It was jealousy.

The penultimate stage of my wish was now in place, so why didn't I feel happy about it? The princess couldn't wait to snatch Ary up and take him off with her. She didn't even wait for him to get dry. By the time we all arrived back at her palace, poor Ary was shivering violently. Some way to treat a hero, I thought huffily. I trailed behind Ary and the princess as she led him to a sumptuous suite of rooms. There was a fire blazing in the hearth with a copper bath sitting before it.

"My poor Sir Aryss," the princess cooed. "I've arranged a hot bath for you. Shall I call a servant to help you disrobe? Or," and her voice dropped suggestively. "Would you like me to help you?"

"I'll be f-f-fine," said Ary through chattering teeth. "I p-prefer to bathe in private."

The princess gave him an arch look. "I certainly didn't get that impression this afternoon," she purred. With a last, pouting look over her shoulder, the princess finally left my wish and I alone.

Ary dragged off his damp clothing and climbed into the bath, sinking down into the water with a groan.

"Remind me never to ride a horse when my britches are wet, Fig," he said. "My arse is rubbed raw."

"Perhaps you can ask the princess to massage it for you," I said nastily.

He lifted an eyebrow and gave me an amused look.

"I'm sure if you just smiled at her like you did this afternoon, she'll be happy to oblige."

"I wasn't smiling at her."

I gave a snort of disbelief.

"I was so sodding cold that my jaw was locked into an expression that might have passed for a smile."

"It *was* a smile."

"You sound a little...jealous, Fig," he said with a grin.

"Well, that's not something I'll have to worry about after tomorrow, is it? No need to be jealous over a dead man."

The moment I spoke, I wished I could take it back. I saw Ary absorb my words like a blow. I saw the pain in his eyes before he lowered his lashes and hid them from me. He sank back in the bath, resting his head against the edge, closing his eyes and shutting me out.

Despite what is said of us in shadow, fairies are not usually deliberately cruel. I had never thought I could be so spiteful. I wanted to tell Ary I was sorry, but the grim set of his mouth froze the words in my throat. Instead, I magicked the bath water to keep it hot, as a small gesture of apology.

Ary kept his eyes closed and, lulled by the warm water and the fire, drifted off to sleep. I crept next to the bath and sat down beside him. The steam had caused his damp hair to curl around his face, but it was his chest that fascinated me. The males of Faerie have no body hair, nothing to mar the sleek, ivory perfection of their skin. Ary's muscled chest was covered with a vee of dark, curling hair and I longed to know how it would feel to run my fingers through it. My hand hovered over his chest, then followed the thin, dark line that trailed down his flat stomach before disappearing beneath the soapy water. I stroked him softly. Of course, I couldn't feel anything, but Ary stirred.

"What are you doing, Fig?" he asked sleepily. He opened his eyes and looked at me, a faint smile curling his lips.

I snatched my hand back guiltily.

"Just checking if the water was still hot."

His smile widened. He raised one hand and drew his fingers down my hair, dripping water on my face.

"Fig," he breathed, leaning towards me and placing his lips against mine. It was like kissing a waterfall, cool and misty, not hot and wet like a kiss was supposed to be. Ary drew back and smiled ruefully. "Not exactly the kiss of your dreams?"

I opened my mouth to tell him that it was the most beautiful kiss I had ever had when the door opened and the princess waltzed in.

"Why, Sir Aryss," she said in surprise. "Still in your bath? Surely the water must be cold by now?" She crossed the room and came and sat in the chair beside Ary's bath, dipping her fingers into the water.

"Still warm!" she said, giving Ary an assessing look. She kept her hand in the water, idly stirring it with her fingers. The woman had an obsession with wet, naked men. Ary watched her hand warily.

"Do you know what it is that you must face tomorrow, Sir Aryss?" the princess asked. "I feel that I must fully inform you of the facts. I wouldn't blame you if you decided to withdraw once you hear the whole sorry tale."

"I won't withdraw," said Ary quietly. "But I would like to know just what I'll be up against."

The princess kept stirring the water as she spoke. "One year ago today, I refused the suit of a prince from the Kingdom of Essen." She made a face. "If you saw him, you'd quite understand why. He was an odious creature, a bare stick of a man and not at all someone to whom I should wish to be married." She ran her eyes appreciatively over Ary's bare chest. Her hand dipped deeper into the water, and Ary gave a startled jerk and drew his knees up tightly against his chest. Water splashed over the side of the bath, soaking the princess's gown. She didn't seem to mind. She gave Ary a knowing smile and pulled her hand out of the water. She ran her hand slowly down the front of her gown, wiping it dry, before continuing.

"Unfortunately, this prince wasn't prepared to take his rejection like a man and decided to be spiteful and draw a curse down upon me. If, one year from the day I spurned his proposal, which by the way is noon tomorrow, I haven't found someone to lift the curse, which by the way is a seventy foot long fire breathing dragon, then I must marry him or the dragon will have me."

Which by the way, I thought, *would not be such a bad thing.*

"So far, seventeen of my most ardent suitors have tested their mettle against this cursed beast and all have fallen. You are my last and best hope, Sir Aryss. If you fail, then I am lost."

"A dragon?" said Ary carefully. "That's not too bad. With Excalibur, I could have a real chance of defeating it." He flashed me a hopeful look.

The princess smiled brightly. "That's exactly what I thought when I saw you come out of that lake today, all wet and...heroic."

That's not all you thought, you fat cow. I was beginning to really dislike this woman.

"There is one more, tinsy winsy thing you should know about this curse," the princess went on.

"Yes?" said Ary warily.

"It's just that...Well, there is another aspect of the curse that you may not like."

"Yes?" said Ary again.

The princess took a deep breath. "When the dragon dies, the one who kills it dies too. It's all rather unfair, I know, but then, curses are never fair, are they? Still, you'll have the consolation of knowing that you died for a noble cause, which by the way, is me."

"I couldn't think of a nobler cause," said Ary dryly. He rested his head on his up drawn knees. The princess reached over and caressed his bare, wet shoulder.

"I feel that some recompense is due you for this sacrifice you are about to make on my behalf," she purred. "Come, Sir Aryss. Let me show you how truly grateful I am." She stood and extended Ary her hand in invitation.

Ary lifted his head and smiled at her. "I fear I must refuse, Highness," he said. "Regretfully, I must spend the night in holy vigil, to prepare my soul for tomorrow's trial."

The princess frowned.

"*Very* regretfully," said Ary firmly.

"If you say so," she said sulkily. "However, surely you won't deny me one kiss, as a token of the vast esteem in which I hold you?"

She didn't give Ary time to say yay or nay, leaning forward and fastening her lips to his. Then she proceeded to practically suck his face off.

When she finally peeled herself off him, she was flushed and breathless. She trailed a finger down Ary's neck.

"Such a wicked waste," she said. She rose to leave. When she reached the door, she looked back at Ary. "If you find that your vigil becomes too wearisome, feel free to come and see me. My room is just up the hall. I'll leave the door unlocked." She blew him a kiss.

Ary sank back down under the water. Feeling decidedly ungracious, I magicked the water again. Ary shot back up, spluttering.

"Jeezus, Fig! Why did you do that?" He pushed himself out of the icy water and, grabbing a towel, began to dry himself vigorously.

"You could have gone with her," I said sulkily. "I wouldn't have cared."

Ary stood still and looked at me. "No, I couldn't," he said sadly. He began to pull on his clothes. When he was dressed, he turned to me and said softly," Will you keep vigil with me tonight, Fig?"

I shook my head miserably, unable to answer for the lump in my throat. Ary's face fell, and he turned away.

"Ary," I finally managed to choke out. "It's not that I don't want to. I *can't*. I can't step foot on hallowed ground."

"I'm not too fond of it myself." He flashed me a sideways smile. "I'll keep vigil here in my room, if you'll stay with me and keep the monsters away."

I nodded, and Ary and I knelt down on the floor. Ary rested Excalibur before him, leaning on the crosspiece of the hilt. Neither of us spoke. I could have knelt there for a hundred years, but Ary shifted about uncomfortably, muttering under his breath. Finally, after several hours, he'd had enough.

"Sod this, Fig," he said wearily. "I'm going to bed." He rose up and moved stiffly to the ornate four poster bed that dominated one side of the room. With a groan, he flung himself face down on the mattress. When he spoke again, his voice was muffled.

"Stay with me, Fig."

I went and lay on the bed beside him. He turned his head and gave me another of his sideways smiles. He lay there with his head on his arms, saying nothing, simply watching me. Eventually, his eyes drifted closed and he fell asleep.

I didn't need to sleep. Nor did I want to. I just wanted to gaze on him for as long as I could. Another thing they say about fairies is that we have no hearts. If that was true, then why was mine breaking into a million pieces?

114

The next morning, we rode with the princess and her host to the dragon's lair. Ary said little as he prepared. He refused the ornate suit of armour the princess offered him.

"I'd prefer to not be roasted alive," he said quietly, choosing instead to don his well-worn cuirass of boiled leather. He hefted Excalibur and gave me a slow, sweet smile. Someone gave him a goblet of wine, and he drank, but I saw that his hands shook.

The place where the dragon roosted was set amidst a tumble of huge boulders that lay scattered across a barren, scorched field. The stench of burnt meat hung heavy in the air and there was a noxious mist that made your eyes water fiercely if you took too deep a breath.

The court set up at the perimeter of the scorched earth, pennons and banners snapping in the brisk winter wind. A tent was erected for Ary to make his final preparations in. He sent away the two squires that came to help him arm, giving me another smile.

"I'd rather see to it myself," he told them.

I watched him as he pulled on a pair of long, leather gauntlets. He flexed his fingers and picked up his sword once more.

"Ready as I'll ever be," he said wryly. Then, so softly that I had to strain to hear him, he asked, "Is it going to be painful?"

"You're going to die a hero's death, Ary," I said hopelessly. "That's always painful."

"Sod it." He gave a rueful grin. "I thought that's what you were going to say."

"Oh, Ary," I whispered. "I wish…"

"Sshh," he placed his fingers against my lips. "Be careful what you wish for. It might come true."

He moved to the entrance of the tent and raised the flap. Looking back over his shoulder, he said, "Goodbye, Fig."

Then he was gone.

My beautiful wish.

My Ary.

I didn't go and watch Ary have his wish granted. I couldn't. Instead, I stayed in the tent, making wishes of my own. Wish after wish. Hundreds of them. Thousands. Over and over and over, hoping that somehow just one of them would be heard. But they weren't. I knew Ary was dead when I felt myself being pulled back through the Vail to Faerie. This time, it did hurt. That's to be expected when you leave a part of yourself behind in shadow.

Back in Faerie, life seemed to go on as it always had. A magical dance of colour and sound and beauty, but to me, it all seemed grey and featureless. Eventually, I managed to drag myself back to the wish bower. After all, that's what I was. A wish fairy.

As soon as I entered, I heard it. My wish. It had been waiting there for me all this time. Hardly daring to believe it, I rushed from the bower and collided with a hard, muscled body. A pair of arms wrapped around me and pressed me against a chest. Warm and solid and oh so real. I lifted my head and my mouth was claimed in a kiss that was as hot and wet and hungry as any kiss is supposed to me.

Be careful what you wish for...because sometimes it might come true.

My mouth was released, and I gazed into a pair of smiling blue eyes.

"Hello, Fig," said Ary.

ANGELO

Elana Gomel

When Angelo was a child, his mother told him that every flower had a fairy. And she described them. Inside the lilac lived a sullen, wizened creature, his face purplish with broken veins. The rose fairy had fanged mouths where her eyes should be. The peony's mistress bristled with tiny iridescent spikes. But when he insisted on seeing them, his mother shook her head. You'll see the fairies when you're old enough, my boy, she said and laughed her sweet, mad laughter.

Angelo's mother died when he was fourteen. One day she left home and went into the fairy forest. She never came back. A week or so later, their yellow mutt slunk into the house with a rag of flesh dangling from his jaws. Angelo watched as the rest of his mother's body, crawling with black ants, was carried in by a couple of village lads, their faces pale with horror. His father hanged himself the next day.

Angelo grew up and became the supreme Judge of the small duchy perched on the borders of the fairy forest. The

Duke respected his rectitude and let him do pretty much whatever he wanted. And what Angelo wanted was to enforce the law. In the country adjacent to the Seelie Court – to say nothing of an occasional raid by the Unseelie Court – the law was the only bulwark against the chaos that threatened to overwhelm man and his works.

The walled town that served as the capital of the duchy stood on the bank of a deep, winding river. Beyond the cleared fields, the mighty forest stretched toward the distant mountains: oaks and birches, and elms, and stands of dark pine shedding needles onto the dusty soil where nothing grew. And worse things – little hollows with miniature lakes, so small that dolls could have sailed them and perhaps dolls did; hills covered with feathery ferns whose stems were red as if dipped in blood; clearings thickly clustered with white and mauve orchids that blossomed all year round, nourished by the decaying flesh of small animals that crawled into the thicket and never came out. It was not certain where the Seelie Court, presided over by Titania and Oberon, was located in this wilderness – provided, of course, that the Seelie Court had any precise location. As for the place of the Unseelie Court, nobody wanted even to speculate.

But wherever they were coming from, fairies never let men be at peace. Mostly, they restricted themselves to silly pranks, like stealing prayer-books or tangling threads on the loom. Sometimes, they would kill a dog or dry a cow's milk. Occasionally, a baby would disappear and the distraught mother would discover a shriveled, mewling thing in the cradle instead. And very occasionally, a woman would be raped or a man castrated.

Angelo succeeded in reviving some of the ancient protective laws that no longer made sense to the decadent inhabitants of the duchy. In particular, they objected to the regulations concerning marital fidelity and sexual purity which, they felt, were uncouth, embarrassing, and unfit for the modern age. But Angelo was relentless in meting out stiff punishments for adulterers and fornicators. He knew what unkind comments were made behind his back, the most printable of which was that he had ice in his veins instead of blood. But he did not care. The force behind his crusade was not prudishness but fear. He did not despise love and planned on getting married in due time. But he saw clearly what his fellow citizens preferred not to know: that desire was the gateway through which the inhabitants of the two Faerie Courts invaded the human world and played havoc with its laws and institutions.

In the course of his research, Angelo discovered an old ordinance that on pain of death prohibited all sexual intercourse for a fortnight before the Midsummer Night's Eve. The Eve was the only truly dangerous time in the duchy. The fairy attacks at that time were as deadly as they were whimsical. In the dusk, a polite stranger, his face masked by a raised cloak, would ask a servant wench for a cup of water and let the cloak slip as he drank it. Next morning, the wench would be a babbling idiot. Or a pretty butterfly would alight on a child and leave him covered with running sores. Or flowers in the garden would pull out their roots and crawl away. Or...there were many ways in which the Seelie Court celebrated the Midsummer Night's Eve, on which date it temporarily reunited with its twin and enemy, the Unseelie Court, under the rule of Titania the Immortal Queen.

Angelo often considered how the dangers of the Eve might be minimized, if not avoided, and an old ordinance suggested a way. Its prescription was blunt: marital intercourse was as unlawful as fornication during these two perilous weeks.

Angelo prepared his campaign carefully. First, he talked to the Duke. The ruler of the principality was an indolent and cynical man but he was not stupid. He was prepared to back any plan as long as its success would be attributed to him and its failure – to his underlings. He suddenly remembered an important state visit, appointed Angelo his plenipotentiary, and rode away.

Angelo instantly issued a proclamation that was greeted exactly as he expected it to be greeted. Not to be deterred by ribald laughter, he ordered all adults to attend daily lectures, prayer vigils and meditation workshops delivered by the armed constabulary. This kept them out of mischief at daytime. But even constables needed to sleep, and so policing every bedroom in the duchy, to say nothing of lofts, basements and haystacks, was out of the question. To enforce his law, Angelo needed to make an example of a transgressor. And a transgressor was conveniently found.

It was a foolish young man named Claudio who seduced his cousin Juliet. The lovers were taken *in flagrante delicto* and the girl was found to be with child. This solved another problem: Angelo felt queasy at the thought of executing a woman. He happily sent bawling Juliet home and jailed Claudio, ordering the gallows to be erected posthaste. However, he did not foresee the petitions, protests, delegations of dignitaries, attempted bribes, and death threats, all of which forced him to postpone the execution until the day of summer solstice.

Finally, the delegations were turned away, the petitions denied, the death threats investigated and dealt with, and Angelo could relax. He decided to reward himself by spending the Midsummer Night in his study, poring over his precious volumes of the Roman law. He knew he deserved a break. What he did not know was that the condemned man had a sister.

Isabella grew up playing with fairies in her father's garden. Tiny creatures with faces of wizened old men and

121

gaudy wings had alighted on her shoulder and whispered strange stories in her ear. By now, she no longer remembered these stories, and her fairy companions had not visited her in a long time. But their dreamlike presence had stamped her with a kind of wholeness that only animals and very small children possess. She ate when she was hungry, and slept when she was tired, and obeyed no law but that of her own nature.

She bribed a couple of guards and positioned herself at the door of Angelo's study. When she heard him get up and walk around to stretch his legs, she pushed the door open and entered.

They had never seen each other before. Isabella was being educated in a convent and had only heard of her younger brother's impending execution ten hours earlier. She had spent eight of them riding back home. She had stolen the horse because Mother Superior would not let her go alone in the middle of the night. She was surprised and pleased that the Judge was not much older than herself and quite attractive. It made her task easier.

She dropped off her heavy cloak and stepped forth naked.

"If you release my brother," she said, "I'll sleep with you."

Angelo yelped and grabbed the dagger he always kept under his legal volumes. The duchy's outraged libertarians had made some half-hearted attempts on his life before. But he let the dagger drop when he saw what was in front of him. The hussy was as naked as the day she was born and as innocent of implements of murder.

"Cover yourself up!" he commanded. "Who let you in?"

She made no move to pick up her cloak and stared at him with a perplexed expression. Surprisingly, he liked her longish face with large brown eyes. He remembered the old superstition that one could recognize a fairy sending because the unusual color of its eyes would betray what material was used to fashion it. But her eyes were warm, common, and human.

"Cover yourself up!" he said again, a little more gently.

Still, she did not move. Angelo sighed. There was no need to prolong this awkward situation and test his own fortitude, which he knew to be considerable but not unlimited. He lifted her cloak and wrapped it around her.

"Who are you?" he asked. "And why do you think I want to sleep with you?"

Isabella was stunned. Because she did not really understand other people but had to adapt to their ways to get what she wanted, she had trained herself to read their intonations and facial expressions and had become quite adept at that. She could tell that the man was not faking. He really was not interested!

"Do you not find me desirable?" she asked in her dulcet voice. The Judge frowned.

"The whole situation is highly improper," he said. "You should not be here at all. Let me call the guards and they'll escort you safely home."

"But why?" Isabella asked innocently. "You make love to me and let my brother go. This is simple and natural."

Angelo's rage at this insult to the law boiled over.

"You're a strumpet!" he snarled. "Your brother will hang tomorrow, and if you're not careful, you'll follow! Get out now!"

Isabella's hand flew to her mouth. The realization that her beauty was impotent to get her what she wanted shook her more than the Judge's threat and her brother's impending death. She backed off clumsily, tripped, and fell. The cloak slipped off again but now her nakedness had the additional – and unintended - appeal of helplessness.

Angelo sighed.

"I cannot let your brother go! Don't you understand? He and this idiot paramour of his have opened the gates to the Two Courts. The Seelie and the Unseelie both are waiting on our borders! If they don't get their sacrifice, they'll destroy us! Are you willing to let it happen? Are you willing to unleash the Wild Hunt on our men, women and children?"

Isabella lifted herself to her knees and smiled at him. Her self-confidence reasserted itself. She was not afraid of the Wild Hunt, and she lacked the imagination to be affected by others' fears.

"I'll go and bargain with the Two Courts myself," she announced. "The Queen, they say, values women more than men; she won't refuse. And then you can temper the harshness of the law with the sweetness of mercy and let my brother go."

Angelo was speechless. This was suicide. No one could go into the fairy forest on the Midsummer Night and come back alive. Such corpses as were recovered bore terrible mutilations. And this strumpet actually offered to suffer such a fate for her no-good brother!

Seeing confusion on his face, Isabella, still kneeling, reached out and put her narrow hand on his thigh – the move that brought the rest of her anatomy too close for comfort. Angelo shook her off and retreated behind his desk.

"I can't let you go!" he muttered. "Your blood will be on

my head!"

"Is it better to have my brother's blood on your head?"

There were many answers he could make but suddenly the entire situation appeared to him embarrassing, compromising, and altogether intolerable. What if one of his scribes suddenly walked in and discovered a stark-naked woman in his study? He would never live it down!

"Go, then!" he declared irritably. "If you make a bargain with the Two Courts, I'll pardon your brother. More likely that your parents are going to mourn two children instead of one but this is your own doing! Get up, make yourself decent, and leave. Go!"

Isabella went back home well pleased with herself. It was late afternoon, and it did not leave her much time to prepare, but she had boundless confidence in her own ability to face down the fairies, get her brother released, and achieve the life of ease, power, and plenty that was her due.

Juliet was sobbing in her room, and Isabella yelled at her to shut up as she went around ordering her maids to draw a bath and to prepare the clothes she needed. Her mother hovered at her door for a while but went away without asking any questions. Claudio was her second child, but sometimes when she looked at her daughter's bright, impenetrable face, she felt he was the only one.

Isabella admired herself in the mirror. The memory of the Judge's rejection cast a fleeting shadow on the polished surface of her mind, but her beauty banished it. Her clothes were just right: a court dress of black velvet with ruffles of antique lace at the low-cut bodice; rubies around her throat and in her ears; and the white froth of fretted petticoats under the hooped over-skirt. Most people would consider it a strange outfit for blundering around in the night forest but she knew better. Titania was the Queen of air and darkness and had to be treated as royalty. She was convinced that the Seelie and Unseelie courts would appreciate the wisdom of her choosing the colors of their dominion: white, red, and black. Many years ago, the fairies in her father's garden had prophesized that she would grow up into these colors: her skin as white as snow, her lips as red as blood, her hair as black as a raven's wing. When she walked out into the warmth of the late afternoon, hobbling a little awkwardly on her high heels, it occurred to her that she was already grown up and her hair was blond, her lips pink, and her skin the color of skin. But she did not dwell on it.

Angelo's evening was irrevocably spoiled. He tried to concentrate on the law of primogeniture but the outrageous image of the strumpet insinuated itself between him and the fine print. He sighed and closed the book. He was a man; he conceded as much. It was not his fault that he was subject to the same desires and temptations as any other man. He thought that perhaps he should visit Mariana. She was the woman he intended to marry someday.

But as he locked the door of his study (too late, he thought sourly), he realized that he did not want to see Mariana. And he also realized that his unease was not desire, which he had learnt from long experience to manage as necessary. It was guilt, and he did not know how to manage it.

The woman was going into the fairy forest on Midsummer Night. She was as good as dead. And he had allowed this; no, he had encouraged her.

He went back home and tried to drink but the rare Spanish wine tasted like vomit. Outside, the summer sky was growing deeper, the gold of the sun changing to copper, the shadows of the trees clawing the ground.

Abruptly, Angelo pushed open the casement and leaned out. There were no flowers in his gardens, just smooth turf and rocks.

Looking into the garden, Angelo thought that perhaps flowers were not the only things that housed fairies. Perhaps everything did. The scum on the pond might hide a creature with a smooth, featureless face the color of moldy bread. The decorative rocks might be alive with tiny, crawling bodies. The velvety lawn might hunch up into the shape of an emerald cat.

And why not human bodies? Perhaps there was a being in his stomach, a purple and yellow ball of slime. Perhaps his limbs were meat-puppets jerked for the amusement of an invisible puppeteer. Perhaps the thing between his legs was a blind leech with a mind of its own.

Angelo suddenly remembered Isabella's narrow, delicate hand. And then he imagined this hand lying in the grass and crawling with black ants.

He took off his court clothes, put on a nondescript dark doublet and a cloak, grabbed a dagger, and went out.

The forest was sleepy and purring like a ginger tomcat, golden-striped by the last rays of the setting sun. Isabella looked around for a fairy messenger that would take her to Titania's court, but the forest appeared to be empty. It was strange.

Isabella's eyes fell onto a thorny black bush that grew by the side of the path. It was leafless and bore shriveled black buds. She touched it, curious why it looked so winter-bare at the height of summer. A curved thorn bit into her palm. She cried out and sucked on the wound but it was too late; drops of her blood rained upon the buds which instantly expanded and burst open, unfolding into giant white flowers with sword-like stamens. The flowers smelled of rot.

"Take me to the Queen!" Isabella cried, trying to still a quiver in her voice.

The dead-white fire of the blossoms consumed the bush, each flower exploding with new petals into a bristling ball. Adjacent blossoms attacked each other, their stamens swinging and clashing like swords at a tournament. With miraculous speed, the empty bark collapsed in upon itself, sucked dry by the voracious flowers that bit into each other with petal-rimmed maws. One of them, more predatory than the rest, consumed its brethren and swelled until it was almost the size of Isabella. As she backed off, the giant flower swiveled and pointed its sharp stamen at her.

"Take me to the Queen!" she repeated.

The thick petals flowed together, and the flower-ball became a mound of mock-flesh that quickly shaped itself into an eidolon. The creature tottered upright, opened its bulging eyes and looked at her. Its irises were the color of abattoir.

Isabella gulped; the sending was animated by her own blood and would follow her, begging for more. This was bad enough but the sending's shape was worse. Its pallid body was long and lean; its head shiny and bald; its mouth – a gaping hole fringed with twitching petals. The sword-stamen stuck out obscenely at its crotch.

Isabella felt bile rise in her throat. She had seen enough animal couplings to develop a matter-of-fact attitude to the procedure. But this…this *thing* was simultaneously threatening and vulgar, a stuff of shameful nightmares. And it had fed on her blood!

She retreated; the sending moved toward her. Desperately, she recalled the innocent companions of her childhood, but they seemed faded and far away.

She turned and ran, sobbing, through the thicket of chokeberry, velvet, lace, and taffeta being shredded by thorny branches. The creature glided after her at a leisurely pace. Its stamen-penis blossomed with curved bone hooks.

For the first time, Angelo entered the fairy forest. It was dipped in slimy light. Scant sunshine oozed down into the black earth that squelched under his feet. He gritted his teeth and persevered. His mind was filled with terrible images of Isabella raped, tortured, or dead. He strained his ears for screams of pain but heard only a remote murmur of trees.

Suddenly, something touched his leg. He jumped up and stifled a scream when he saw what it was. A little girl grasped the top of his boot with a tiny, dimpled hand.

Angelo backed off slowly, mindful of the Seelie (or was it the Unseelie?) penchant for cruel tricks. The toddler's face scrunched up, and she emitted a thin desperate wail. Then she plumped down among the tussocks of grass and started crying in earnest. She was wearing a dirty smock and one baby shoe.

Angelo hesitated. It was one of his best-kept secrets that he had a soft spot for cats and small children. And what if this was a real baby and not a fairy eidolon? Child-stealing was a specialty of the Unseelie Court, and it did happen that they lost interest and abandoned their prey in the woods.

Cautiously, he approached the wailing girl and picked her up. She stopped crying and tearfully smiled at him. She was a pretty baby with curly hair and round face. There was a long, shallow scratch on her cheek, dry blood and dust matting her soft skin. Unthinkingly, Angelo moistened the edge of his cloak with his saliva and tried to rub it off.

Branches whipped Isabella's face as she tore through the brambles and undergrowth in blind panic. Her beautiful clothes hung in tatters; her hair was full of leaves and twigs; and her feet – she had lost her slippers – bled. But she hardly felt any pain. What she felt was the helplessness of a small, hunted animal.

Suddenly, the ground disappeared from under her feet. She stumbled, fell, and rolled down a grassy slope. She ended up flat on her back. Opening her eyes, she saw the pink sky with a single silvery star hanging low and the sunset clouds still smoldering above the treetops. Then she discovered she was lying in a small hollow cupped between gentle hills. It was fringed by a stand of aspens and thickly grown with tiny ferns.

Unsteadily, Isabella got to her feet. The panic had subsided and its place was taken by burning shame at her failure. All she wanted now was to escape the forest, crawl back home, and hide under the blanket without seeing another human being - ever. But as she was untying the strings that attached the broken hoops of her over-skirt to the bodice, she realized that among the people she was never going to see was Claudio. She had wanted to best Angelo more than she had wanted to save her brother. But now, tears came, and they were for him.

Suddenly, there was a rustle above her. The aspens parted and the white sending slipped through, shining with a pale glow. Its penis was now a spiny, writhing snake.

Isabella looked around but there was nowhere to run. The snake hissed and reared.

And suddenly, the voice of Mother Superior reading from a book on rhetoric rang in her ears. She had never taken her convent education seriously, but she knew it was the necessary stepping-stone toward her ultimate goal and consequently, she was quite good at it. She faced the sending.

"I'm a pure virgin," she declared grandly. "Is this how you show your respect?"

The sending cocked its head. Isabella remembered the garden fairies' stories and songs, simple and straightforward like the prattle of children. Surely creatures like these had no defense against the wiles of legalism!

"You have tasted my blood, have you not?" she asked sternly.

The sending nodded a tiny, hesitant nod.

"This makes me your blood sister and thus prohibited to you under any condition. You may not even gaze at my nakedness under the penalty of ten strokes with a birch whip or temporary blindness. Both the Seelie and the Unseelie Courts recognize blood brotherhood and King Bronwen of the Unseelie and Queen Bramwen of the Seelie were blood brother and sister."

This much was true or at least a commonly told tale. The rest Isabella was making up as she went on. But would a sending made of bark, blossom and blood know any better?

"You have uncovered your sister's nakedness," Isabella continued, warming up to her theme. "If you are of the Seelie, of the Bright Court, you shall pay me restitution. If you are of the Unseelie, of the Dark Court, you shall be my slave for ten years. But since tonight, of all nights, the two courts unite, you shall do both."

The creature's snake-penis drooped and shrunk. Isabella drew herself upright.

"Are you willing to do my bidding?" she asked severely. "Or shall I drag you before Queen Titania herself, the sovereign ruler of the Two Courts?"

The creature trembled and shed petals into the grass. Isabella reminded herself to go easy on it; she did not want to frighten it out of existence. She needed it for a job.

"If you do exactly as I say," she said, "I shall forgo the ten-year slavery."

The creature nodded energetically. Its crotch was now pristinely smooth.

"Well, come here," said Isabella, "and listen carefully…"

The moment Angelo's cloak moistened with his spittle touched the girl's filthy cheek, he knew it was a terrible idea. He could not believe he had made this stupid mistake when every child in the duchy knew that one should never let the Good Folk have anything that comes out of one's body, be it hair, nail parings, saliva, urine, semen, or blood. But the Judge often preferred to forget that he had a body which exuded various shameful substances, and being always clean himself, he could not abide dirt in others.

He jerked his hand away and dropped the girl. But it was too late. Her eyes blinked and milky whiteness flowed through them, filling them to the brim and spilling over onto her cheeks. Her smile did not waver, though. It just grew and grew as her lips stretched across her face, dividing her head into two. The upper part flipped off like the lid of a boiling pot and foamy white liquid poured out. Angelo gagged and turned around to flee.

But the girl was now in front of him, as if there were two of them, and perhaps there were but he did not dare look back. Only she was not a girl anymore. She had expanded into a woman-size figure, exaggeratedly feminine, with high breasts and a tiny waist, molded of runny mucus. This nauseating parody of a female looked vaguely familiar and to his horror, Angelo recognized her. The Unseelie creature had shaped itself into an obscene likeness of Isabella.

Now he did vomit, though having had little to eat the whole day, he mostly brought up bile. The creature dropped down on all fours, sniffing at the bile. Angelo was frantic with disgust.

The sun had set, but in the white light of the long summer dusk he could see it all with far more clarity than he wanted to. The Isabella thing sat down on its liquefying rump. It lifted its dripping arms to its chest, tugged at it, and twitched its shoulders like a woman getting out of a tight dress. The mucus flesh parted and something even more revolting popped out. A blunt, yellow muzzle pushed out from the slimy cocoon, its swollen tongue hanging like a dark banner. The creature that was being hatched had a dog's head and a woman's body. It was crawling with black ants that streamed out from its eyes like a child's clumsy drawing of tears. But the eyes themselves were glistening white, the color of saliva.

Angelo realized that he was tottering on the edge of insanity. Almost gleefully, he foresaw his own mad lurch through the forest, his clothes torn and filthy, mindless shriek bubbling up from his raw throat.

And just as he visualized this picture in every excruciating detail, he realized how ridiculous it was.

The horror popped like a soap bubble. He wrinkled his nose at the creature's rotten smell. It stared at him expectantly.

"You poor thing!" said Angelo and patted the creature's wet, matted fur.

"There are," said Titania to Oberon, her lord, "three

ways to please a mortal woman. Unfortunately, nobody knows what they are."

Her lord did not answer. He had been dead for a year. His body had become a hatchery for young fairies that swarmed in the rotting flesh, emerging from luminous larvae. One fairy fluttered upwards and perched on Titania's outstretched, four-fingered hand. The second hand, made into a fist, hung down by the queen's scaly side.

The sprite had the muzzle of a weasel and the body of a boy. The queen of the Two Courts bent her head to look at the new creature. Her head was that of a giant crow, its faded black feathers scuffed on top where a golden crown had previously rested. Now the crown was placed on the mossy hillock and worked over by a crew of dung beetles. They were removing the rubies and emeralds from their settings and substituting dead men's eyes instead.

"Look at them," said Titania to the sprite. "Humans can be so funny!"

She opened her fist. The elongated palm was fringed with a strip of trembling gray-green filaments and in the middle of it moved two pale ticks.

"Poor clumsy creatures," said Titania, her beak opening wide in a yawn.

The dog-headed sending persisted in trotting after Angelo. It was rather clumsy, and its smell did not make it a pleasant companion either. But he did not have the heart to shoo it away. He remembered having read somewhere that sendings only survived for a short time. Perhaps being close to the source of its existence would give the creature a longer lease on life. Previously, he would have asked himself what was the use of such a life but he did not now.

The sky was luminous but the ground was mantled with shadows. Angelo ripped his cloak to shreds when it caught on a pine branch and skinned his knee on a boulder. But he persevered. He had to find Isabella. Clearly the dangers of the Two Courts were to the mind rather than to the body, but how would a weak woman withstand an assault of guilty nightmares?

There was a stand of aspens ahead of him, their delicate trembling canopies etched in black against the whiteness of the sky. Something dark and indistinct pushed between two trunks: another fairy or sending in the shape of a woman. Her semi-nude body shone in the twilight.

"Just leave it off, will you?" he yelled at the fairy. "It doesn't work on me!"

The fairy started, and he realized he was being boorish.

"I'm sorry, Good Neighbor," he said, softening his tone. "I meant no disrespect. I'm looking for a woman who has been lost in your kingdom. Lead me to her and we'll both leave you to your...hmm, celebrations."

"Angelo?" said the fairy in amazement.

"How do they mate with all these skins on?" asked the weasel-headed sprite. "Do they shed them like snakes?"

Other fairies meanwhile had joined the audience. There was a double-bodied girl, with two pale trunks joined by a single head, a golden pince-nez perched askew on her nose. There was a colony of squirming pink worms interlaced together into a rough simulacrum of a human shape. There was a small, peaky child whose twin brother grew out of his chest.

"The males have these sharp implements," said the

double-bodied girl authoritatively, "and they cut through their partners' shells."

"No, they tear them off," hissed the worms in unison, sounding like a man with a bad cold.

"The eggs hatch from within and break the shells," corrected Titania.

It was twilight now, the endless fairy dusk, the fifth time of day. The sky was gray and soft like a dove's breast. They were huddling together in the hollow. The grass was studded with the radiant cups of night-flowers. Shiny worms with human faces crawled on the ground and moths as big as sparrows flapped in the balmy air.

"I still can't believe you followed me here," Isabella said.

Angelo had spread the remnants of his cloak for her to sit on, but she insisted he should sit by her side, and he was painfully aware of her smooth shoulder touching his.

"I couldn't let you die in the Two Courts," he said.

She turned her head to look at him, her hair falling across his face.

"I think we all die in the Two Courts," she said.

"What do you mean?"

"I was very frightened at first. But then I realized there is nothing to be afraid of because we carry our own Courts with us all the time. Day and night; birth and death; water and blood. This is all we are."

"I hope we're more than that," Angelo said, scandalized. "I have an immortal soul. I'm sure you do too."

Isabella laughed softly and stroked his cheek. Angelo

opened his mouth to protest but Isabella's grubby fingers landed on his lips, so he kissed them instead.

"Now," Titania said with some satisfaction, "they are going to mate."

A gaggle of flower fairies surrounded her now, perched on her mighty shoulders, fluttering in the air around her head or clinging to the trees. They were delicate semi-transparent creatures, their bodies and gauzy wings colored according to their flower.

Titania held her hand rigidly outstretched, and in its hollow, the lovers were kissing.

"They're like doves," said the double-bodied girl. "So sweet!"

"Doves are good to eat," the worms hissed.

"It's so boring!" complained the child with a twin.

Titania grabbed the weasel-fairy with her free hand, bit off his head and slurped the stream of blood that jetted from the neck. The smell of blood drove several flower fairies into feeding frenzy, and they buzzed around her until she swatted them.

Dropping the headless body, Titania focused her cartwheel eyes on the lovers.

"It's taking them too long," she grumbled.

"When will she whelp?" the turquoise bluebell fairy hummed.

"She has to lay eggs first," the double-bodied girl explained.

"You're so smart!" exclaimed the bluebell fairy in

admiration.

"Will she eat him afterwards?" the pink dog-rose fairy asked.

"No chance," the yellow daisy fairy grumbled.

The peaky child grabbed the bluebell fairy and fed her to his twin.

"Be done, be done!" Titania cried impatiently. "What's so special about you? Dog and cats do it; and flies and beetles too! Hurry!"

"It's making me nervous," the daisy fairy complained.

She reached inside herself and pulled out a skein of tangled intestines. Spreading them into a dripping web, she flew toward a large beech tree that hummed softly to itself. A flock of tiny cherubic babies with greenish lanterns fluttered in and out of the tree's canopy. Several of them blundered into the daisy fairy's web and got stuck. She hauled the web with its catch back into her belly, and it snapped shut with a wet sound.

"Are they still looking for the right appendages?" the worms hissed.

The double-bodied girl shivered.

"There is something in the air…" she whispered. Her two bodies threw their arms around each other as if looking for shelter. A shudder passed through Titania's giant bulk, and the whole forest trembled, leaves raining down on the grass. Oberon's decaying corpse split in the middle, and a great mass of fairy larvae plopped out.

"I wish they stop!" cried Titania in distress.

The peaky child with a twin caught another flower fairy.

"It'll be over soon," he said, baring his small, pointed teeth. "They mated. She will bear young. He will kill them, so he can mate again. Death and life, life and death, the Two Courts together. There is nothing else."

"Who are you to teach us?" the double-bodied girl screamed at him in sudden fury. "Rot-eater! All of you, Unseelie buggers, you're mulch!"

She snatched her pince-nez and pitched it at the boy. But her aim went awry because the second body tried to stop the attack. Instead of hitting him, the pince-nez smacked into the dog-rose fairy and brought her down. The fairy, helplessly twitching on the grass, was immediately attacked by the dung beetles who had run out of the eyes for Titania's crown. The dog-rose fairy was quickly dismembered and carried away. The worms tittered.

"Oh, shut up, all of you!" cried the fairy queen. "I should not have allowed this to happen! And now I can't make it stop!"

There was an acrid smell of burning in the air. The lush grass of the fairy clearing was turning brown as if singed by invisible flame. The flowers dotting the ground writhed in distress. A large poppy swayed wildly as its scarlet cup filled with smoke. One by one, the flowers caught fire.

"Stop it!" Titania wailed. "What do you want from us? Why do you have to come to the Two Courts and burn them to the ground?"

The double-bodied girl, trying to comfort the frightened worms, hugged them so tightly with her four arms that the colony disintegrated and its components wriggled away in panic. The peaky child's twin broke away and crawled after them, snapping at the stragglers.

With a moan of pain, Titania grasped her beak and tore off her bird face. Underneath there was the muzzle of a gray fox, its teeth bared in a grimace of defiance. The fairy larvae milling at her feet cried out in plaintive voices.

Titania was clawing at her faces, peeling them off and tossing them onto the heaving ground. A she-wolf, a sheep, a writhing sea anemone, an earwig, a chimp, a clump of rose petals, a snake with human eyes, a woman with a forget-me-not growing out of each eye socket...She was screaming, a high-pitched, monotonous sound. The towering mass of her body shook uncontrollably. But the hand in which she held the lovers was rigid, defying the chaos that now spread to all the inhabitants of the Two Courts.

The last face was blank. Swaying over the devastation of her kingdom, Titania put all her remaining strength into bending her fingers. Slowly, she closed her fist.

"Yes!" Titania cried in triumph.

But even as the word left her lips, a quick tongue of fire leapt out, licked her scaly forearm, ran up to the shoulder, smoldered in the dark feathers of her head. Wreathed in flame, Titania became a giant torch illuminating the ruins of the fairyland. She burnt over the debris of magic as the sky darkened into the night and the moon rose peacefully into the dark sky.

Some tenacious root was digging into Isabella's back. The air was getting colder, the ground lumpier, and then a gust of wind brought the pungent smell of smoke.

They jumped up and saw that among the trees a small fire was burning. Angelo beat it down with Isabella's petticoat. Peering at the dying embers, he saw a scatter of tiny bodies among the jerking shadows. He thought they were insects and mites until he made out the contorted shapes of their multiform agony.

"Did you see it?" he asked Isabella. "I mean, when we were..."

"Yes," she said. "I saw."

She had seen indeed, in snatches of vision, on periphery of her pleasure: the luminescent sky swarming with angelic insects, and the animal paw, larger than the hand of God, holding them under the scrutiny of an animal eye. She had felt the air ignite and the earth tremble. And now there were scorch marks on her petticoat.

"We destroyed the Two Courts," he said, puzzled. "How? Why?"

"We broke the law," said Isabella, "and the poor creatures were shocked to death."

"Law? The fairies are denizens of chaos. They have no law."

"Wrong. Nothing is as law-abiding as the wild things. They have to eat, to breed, and to die. We are free to make the law or to break it."

"This is sophistry," he muttered.

She shrugged.

"Suit yourself."

He offered her his arm, and they walked out of the forest in silence. When they were nearing the outskirts of the town, Angelo spoke.

"I'll release your brother, of course," he said, clearing his throat. "I cannot execute a man for a crime I'm guilty of myself. Anyway, the danger to the duchy seems to have been averted."

"Oh no!" Isabella exclaimed.

"What?"

"I sent a…well, a messenger to the jail. Claudio must be home already."

"The guards won't release anybody without my personal

order."

"It *was* your personal order," Isabella confessed. "I made it...the sending...in your image."

"How could you do it?"

"It's not hard if you can visualize the person clearly. And I... I remembered your face well."

Angelo opened his mouth to deliver a stinging rebuke and closed it again.

They came to the gate of Isabella's family mansion. The gate was open, the windows lit, and the sounds of cheering spilled out into the street. The sending had apparently done its job.

"Well," Angelo muttered, avoiding her eyes, "it's a little too late now, and your family must be celebrating Claudio's return, so I'll postpone my conversation with your father till tomorrow morning. It's more seemly this way."

"Conversation?"

"I mean my suit. Asking for your hand in marriage."

"What?" Isabella stared at him in consternation. "I can't marry you! I have other plans!"

And indeed, when the Duke came back from his state visit, Isabella married him. Angelo married Mariana who had been patiently waiting for him in her moated grange. The Duchess had been known to refer to the Judge's wife rather unkindly as "this whey-faced bitch." But despite this tension among the mighty, the town prospered, untroubled by incursions from the Two Courts. Everybody agreed that this was due to the secret ritual of powerful magic performed annually by the Duchess and the Supreme Judge as they solemnly walked into the fairy forest every Midsummer Night's Eve and returned at dawn.

www.ingramcontent.com/pod-product-compliance
Lightning Source LLC
Chambersburg PA
CBHW070749120626
46557CB00002B/516